Rouletabille
at Krupp's

IN THE SAME SERIES

Rouletabille and the Mystery of the Yellow Room
(translated by J.-M. & R. Lofficier)

ALSO BY GASTON LEROUX

The Phantom of the Opera
(translated by J.-M. & R. Lofficier)

Rouletabille
at Krupp's

by
Gaston Leroux

translated, annotated and introduced by
Brian Stableford

A Black Coat Press Book

ISBN 978-1-61227-144-6. First Printing. February 2013. Published by Black Coat Press, an imprint of Hollywood Comics.com, LLC, P.O. Box 17270, Encino, CA 91416.

Introduction

Rouletabille chez Krupp, here translated as *Rouletabille at Krupp's*, was originally published as a seven-part serial in the monthly magazine *Je Sais Tout* between September 1917 and March 1918, and was reprinted in book form by Pierre Lafitte in 1920. It was the fifth novel featuring Rouletabille that Gaston Leroux had penned, although it became the sixth in volume form because one of the earlier ones was split into two for book publication. It differed from its predecessors, however, in three significant respects, all of which give it a particular historical interest. Firstly, it is the only novel in the series to embody a significant science-fictional component, in its depiction and description of a kind of "ultimate weapon" allegedly so powerful as to potentially capable of putting an end to war. Secondly, it is the only one in which Rouletabille features as a secret agent commissioned by the French government to carry out a covert mission in enemy territory, and it thus became one of the significant pioneering examples of that kind of spy fiction. Thirdly, it is the only novel in the series calculated to serve as morale-building propaganda, and was at least encouraged in its production and publication, if not formally commissioned, by the French Ministry of War.

Publication of fiction in France had, inevitably, been severely impeded by the outbreak of the Great War in August 1914, not merely because of the general economic disruption and paper shortages, but because reading fiction—especially fanciful fiction—came to be seen, by the authorities and the public alike, as something essentially frivolous and unbecoming. The kind of reading often described as "escapism," can seem, at first glance, to be inappropriate in wartime, almost as a kind of "mental desertion" from more serious and purposive concerns. Such fiction as continued to be published in France in 1915 tended to be deadly earnest in its form and concerns, and determinedly naturalistic. The relatively small number of magazines that continued to publish fiction mostly confined their efforts to stories of life in the trenches, blatantly calculated to raise morale by celebrating the everyday heroism of conscripts in the face of routine tribulations. It was not the case that all fiction published in that year was lightly-disguised propaganda, but most of the fiction intended for mass consumption was.

In 1916, however, this situation eased somewhat, and in 1917 it appears to have undergone a definite shift, not with respect to the fundamental propagandistic purposes of the fiction published, but with respect to its narrative strategies. In part, this represented a belated realization that "escapism" is not such a bad thing in wartime, because readers might benefit, even more in peacetime, from a temporary release from the pressures of grim reality, and also a realization that the narrative force of "gripping" fiction can be recruited to the purpose of morale-building in a quasi-inspirational fashion. Kinds of fiction that had become scarce in France in 1915, including action/adventure fiction, historical fiction, crime fiction and science fiction, began to appear in greater quantities again in 1916, usually with a naked propagandistic slant, but also with a much higher priority on entertainment value, and with a much greater imaginative range. After relatively tentative beginnings in that year, there was a noticeable surge in the publication of such works in 1917, although many had obviously been written earlier or separately, and had been hastily adapted to the new regime.

Among the more imaginatively-adventurous novels published in 1917, Félicien Champsaur's *Les Ailes de l'Homme* [1] had obviously been written as an item of futuristic fiction prior to August 1914 and had had to be awkwardly adapted and augmented; while J. H. Rosny's *L'Enigme de Givreuse* [2] simply has an entirely gratuitous chapter in which the protagonist attacks a German submarine dropped into an item of philosophical speculative fiction typical of the author's work in that vein. *Rouletabille chez Krupp*, by contrast, was clearly conceived and executed entirely within the new program, with its purposes in mind. It was published in the leading Parisian popular magazine of the day, and warrants consideration as one of the central texts of the morale-boosting project.

If any such fiction was directly commissioned by the Ministry of War, Gaston Leroux would have been at or very near the top of the list of potential conscripts for such war work, as one of the most successful *feuilletonistes* of the period. Although, like all the other professional writers in France, he had had a very lean time in 1915, when he published no fiction at all, he had resumed duty as a *feuilletoniste* for the daily *Le Matin* in 1916, when he had published the 31-part *Confitou* in January and February and the 135-part *La Colonne infernale* [The Infernal Column] between April and Sep-

---

[1] Available in a Black Coat Press edition as *The Human Arrow*, ISBN 978-1-61227-045-6.
[2] Available in a Black Coat Press edition as *The Givreuse Enigma*, ISBN 978-1-935558-39-2.

tember. The latter might have been one of the texts prompting the change of official policy, and *Le Matin* published another 134-part serial, *Le Sous-marin "Le Vengeur"* [The Submarine *Le Vengeur*] between September 1917 and February 1918. The early episodes of the latter work were published in parallel with *Rouletabille chez Krupp*, but the latter must be reckoned the earlier work, even if the production of the serials overlapped, because of the longer publication-lag to which *Je Sais Tout* was subject.[3] Leroux had also published an eight-part serial in *Je Sais Tout* between June 1916 and January 1917, *L'Homme qui revient de loin* [The Man Who Came Back from Afar].

Rouletabille chez Krupp was by no means the first French *roman scientifique* to feature a weapon so dreadful as to be allegedly capable of putting an end to war. Indeed, that notion had been a standard feature of French futuristic speculation since 1840, although standards of dreadfulness had been considerably inflated in the interim, and more pessimistically-inclined writers had began to suspect, if not to take it for granted, that no matter how destructive a weapon might be, military men would be only too keen to use it, even at the cost of the annihilation of civilization, or the entire human species. Given the circumstances of its production, however, Leroux's

---

[3] *Le Sous-marin "le Vengeur"* was split into two volumes for book publication by Lafitte in 1920, where it bore the collective title of *Aventures effroyables de M. Herbert de Renich* [The Frightful Adventures of Herbert de Renich], and the individual volumes were entitled *Le Capitaine Hyx* [Captain Hyx] and *La Bataille invisible* [The Invisible Battle]. The two volumes were translated into English, rather confusingly, as *The Adventures of Carolus Herbert* and *The Veiled Prisoner*.

novel could not actually depict the deployment of the weapon in question, but had to employ it as an apocalyptic threat whose use against France had to be prevented—a necessity that compelled him to invent, or at least to sophisticate, a formula that was bound to become one of the standard tropes of 20th century spy fiction, which is replete with apocalyptic threats in urgent need of being thwarted by ingenious heroism.

Rouletabille had begun his fictional career as a detective in the tradition of Sherlock Holmes, using the power of logic to solve seemingly-intractable problems—his first adventure, *Le Mystère de la chambre jaune* (1907)[4] remains famous as the first significant "locked room mystery"—but the fundamental narrative purpose of *Rouletabille chez Krupp* forced the hero into a new mold, as the ultimate prototype of James Bond. Although he still retained his commitment to careful observation and ratiocination, he became a much more proactive protagonist, not merely a solver of mysteries thrown at him by happenstance but an *agent provocateur*, making things happen and employing his ingenuity to carry out subversive activities under the protection of an assumed identity.

Leroux did not invent spy fiction as such, but in terms of the modern embryology of the genre, he was certainly acquainted with the man who did, who had, like him, worked as a foreign correspondent for a major newspaper in the decade prior to the Great War: the French-born English journalist William le Queux.

---

[4] Available in a Black Coat Press edition as *Rouletabille and the Mystery of the Yellow Room*, ISBN 978-1-934543-60-3.

Because the Great War had been anticipated for such a long time, and fear of the German war machine had been rife in both England and France ever since its spectacular triumph in the Franco-Prussian War of 1870, newspapers in both countries had become very anxious about the possibility that German secret agents might be busy collecting intelligence that might be useful when the war eventually broke out. Le Queux had played a central role in creating the paranoiac mythology of a German "hidden hand" or "fifth column" devoted to such work, and, in his secondary career as a novelist, had begun to embody the notion in such fictional works as *England's Peril* (1899) and *The German Spy* (1914), as well as such supposedly non-fictional tracts as *Spies of the Kaiser* (1909). Like Leroux, Le Queux continued producing propagandistic fiction during the war, including fiction about powerful new weapons, such as *The Zeppelin Destroyer* (1916). His pre-war anxieties had undoubtedly been contagious, although Leroux does not seem to have been infected to any considerable degree until circumstances warranted it, and never wrote the kind of alarmist future war fiction that was Le Queux's chief stock-in-trade.

Le Queux did not have any conspicuous gift for story-telling, and never acquired the kind of popularity as a fiction-writer that Leroux had in France. His spy stories, moreover—like the vast majority of those produced prior to August 1914—usually featured heroic Englishmen accidentally happening upon and subsequently thwarting the dastardly schemes of German secret agents on an *ad hoc* basis. The idea that the English or French governments would or should adopt underhanded intelligence-gathering tactics themselves went largely unvoiced in popular fiction until the ethics of necessity came into play.

If Le Queux is unlikely to have had any influence on the French government's change of policy regarding propaganda fiction, however, one English writer who might well have done so is John Buchan, who wrote one of the war's surprise best-sellers, *The Thirty-Nine Steps* (1915), while impatiently waiting to be sent on active duty. Although that book follows the already-standardized formula in which an English layman, Richard Hannay, is required by unkind circumstance to thwart insidious German spies, Hannay was rapidly conscripted for a much more ambitious project in the much-superior novel *Greenmantle* (1916),[5] in which he became part of a team carrying out an officially-sanctioned dangerous mission in enemy territory.

It was *Greenmantle* that became the key model for the entire subgenre of secret agent fiction, and Leroux was probably aware of its existence before penning *Rouletabille chez Krupp*, although Leroux's novel is very different in style and attitude, shunning the dogged "stiff upper lip" that Buchan displayed and celebrated more than any other British writer in favor of an archetypally French verve and panache. Leroux had, however,

---

[5] *The Thirty-Nine Steps* is nowadays much more famous than *Greenmantle* because of Alfred Hitchcock's classic film—which threw away all but the barest bones of Buchan's lame plot and substituted a much better one—although the latter is a far better book. Leroux suffered a similar fate when the various cinematic and stage adaptations of *Le Fantôme de l'Opéra* (1910; available in a Black Coat Press edition as *The Phantom of the Opera*, ISBN 978-1-932983-13-5) gradually focused his posthumous fame on that single work, eclipsing many that are considerably more interesting as texts.

already anticipated some of the features of the shift toward clever teamwork in the previous Rouletabille novel, *Rouletabille à la guerre* [Rouletabille at War], which began serialization in *Le Matin* in March 1914, although the serialization was interrupted by the outbreak of the war just as it was reaching its climax, and the last half-dozen of its 135 episodes did not appear until October.[6]

The text of *Rouletabille chez Krupp* refers back to the earlier collective adventure several times, usually citing its most significant setting. *Rouletabille à la guerre* was by no means the first action/adventure novel to cash in on the useful formula of a tightly-knit group of heroes working under the supervision of a charismatic leader to accomplish a seemingly-impossible mission, but it was a significant deployment of the narrative move, which provided a robust foundation for *Rouletabille chez Krupp*.

Leroux had not intended Rouletabille to be a series character when he first invented him, and had to introduce significant modifications to his back-story when he decided to write a sequel to *Le Mystère de la chambre jaune* in *Le Parfum de la dame en noir* (1908-09); tr. as *The Perfume of the Woman in Black*). The first novel had been set in 1892 but the second has a near-contemporary setting and refers back to the events of the earlier novel as having been set three years earlier. Chronological confusions continued as Rouletabille became a significant early example of a hero who never

---

[6] *Rouletabille à la guerre* was split into two volumes for book publication by Lafitte in 1916, as *Le Château noir* [The Black Castle] and *Les Étranges noces de Rouletabille* [Rouletabille's Strange Wedding], thus creating the ambiguity as to whether *Rouletabille chez Krupp* is the fifth or sixth item in the series.

got any older, although the world around him aged considerably. He was still a "young reporter" in *Rouletabille chez le tsar* [Rouletabille at the Tsar's] in 1913, and in *Rouletabille chez Krupp* in 1917, reflecting the fact that he was a rather nostalgic as well as heavily idealized projection of the author's own self. In fact, Leroux, who was born in 1868 but only became a professional journalist after the turn of the century, had never been a "young reporter," having spent his youth squandering the fortune he had inherited in riotous living—although that dubious apprenticeship undoubtedly served him well when he did buckle down to serious journalism, in terms of the contacts he had made and the knowledge of life in the fast lane that he had acquired.

Whatever his origins might have been, however—and in fictional terms, they became fearfully complicated in the process of solving the mystery of the yellow room—by 1917, Rouletabille had become one of those larger-than-life characters who acquire a quasi-archetypal status, and he was, in more ways than one, the ideal character to take on the sort of narrative task that the Ministry of War required of propagandistic fiction. It is significant that *Rouletabille chez Krupp*, perhaps more than any other novel produced in the same spirit, sets out to demonize the enemy in a remarkably flamboyant fashion, in the key chapters entitled "Le Maître de feu" (tr. as "The Master of Fire") and "Le Plus Grand Chantage du Monde" (tr. as "The Greater Blackmail of the World"), in which the Krupp armaments factory becomes a transfiguration of Dante's *Inferno*, and Kaiser Wilhelm II appears in person to guide the readers around it, in the person of a metaphorical Satan.

The symbolism of these chapters, in which Rouletabille, quietly masquerading as a fireman in the background of the tour, is juxtaposed with both the Kaiser and the gigantic superweapon, the *Titania*, is decidedly crude, but is perhaps all the more striking because of it. If the story falters thereafter—as it does, to some extent—it is only because the nightmarish quality and bizarre melodrama of the tour and its subsidiary scenes are unsurpassable, and although the bulk of the plot's ingenuity is devoted to the construction and development of their aftermath, its unraveling could hardly help seeming somewhat trivial by comparison. In the same way, the superweapon itself, having made its awesome symbolic appearance in this sequence, is compelled fade away into a curious oblivion, having done its real job—a narrative inevitability regarding which I shall reserve further comment until an afterword, in order not to give too much away in advance about the story.

Seen in retrospect, *Rouletabille chez Krupp* is not the best of the Rouletabille novels—although the later ones, *Le Crime de Rouletabille* [Rouletabille's Crime] (1921) and *Rouletabille chez les Bohémiens* [Rouletabille Among the Gypsies] (1922), continued the decline, and would have completed it had not Rouletabille become one of those characters who outlived his author and featured in numerous adventures by other hands in various formats. It is, however, a particularly interesting inclusion in the canon, making more use of Leroux's fascination with and talent for the bizarre than the other series novels.

It was a novel very much of its moment, and was arguably obsolete before it appeared in book form in 1920, but as a reflection of the imaginative concerns of the French people in 1917 and the revised policy of wartime propaganda that took full effect in that year, it has a stark specificity and punctiliousness that are unmatched.

It requires reading with that historical context in mind, but still makes interesting reading from that perspective.

This translation has been made from the London Library's copy of the Lafitte edition of 1920.

Brian Stableford

Chapter I
Corporal Rouletabille

When Corporal Rouletabille disembarked on the stroke of five p.m. at the Gare de l'Est, he still had the mud of the trenches on his boots, and he strove more vainly than ever, not to rid himself of a glorious clay that scarcely bothered him, but to guess by what magic spell he had been snatched away from his multiple duties as a platoon-leader in a front-line position at Verdun.

He had received an order to go to Paris as quickly as possible and, as soon as he reached the capital, to go to the offices of his paper, *L'Époque*. The whole business seemed to him not merely very mysterious but so "anti-military" that he did not understand it at all.

Even so, in haste as he was to discover the reason for his singular journey, the reporter was glad to walk for a while after long hours spent on the train.

It was the first time he had seen Paris since the outbreak of the war. It was mid-September. The day had been fine. In the oblique rays of sunlight the foliage of the Boulevard de Strasbourg and the Boulevard Magenta was gilded and enflamed, extending its double russet stream toward the heart of Paris. The movement of the city below was full of light and tranquility—just like old times! The young reporter obtained an infinite joy from the sight.

Others before him had come back and had experienced an egotistical pain on seeing the city in its serene pre-war splendor, a few kilometers from the tranches. They had wanted to find a face of suffering in rapport with their own anxieties, anguishes and sacrifices. Rouletabille, however, took a singular pride in it. *It's because I'm out there*, he said to himself, *that it's like this here. Well, that, at least, gives me pleasure. People are confident!*

And he straightened up in his dishevelment, in his muddy garments.

No one even looked at him. Nor did they pay any more attention to the other *poilus* who were coming down the Boulevard de Strasbourg, coming back from the front, trailing around them a whole paraphernalia of the noisy war, any more than they paid attention to those who were going back up to the Gare de l'Est, their leave having ended, ready to go forth and resume their mortal sentry-duty, behind which the city had resumed its respiration, the powerful and calm rhythm of its life as the queen of the world.

At the corner of the great boulevards, Rouletabille stopped momentarily, remembering the frightful tumult of the riotous scenes that had desolated this entire quarter of Paris in the early days of mobilization, when a nervous population thought it saw spies everywhere, and a few hooligans had set forth on looting expeditions.

Now, on the café terraces, around neatly-aligned tables, placid groups of people were taking aperitifs in the mildness of the evening, after the day's labors. *That's pleasing*, Rouletabille thought, *really pleasing! And, as Clemenceau says, the Boche are at Noyon!*[7]

---

[7] Noyon, in the Compiègne, lent its name to two major battles in the Great War subsequent to the writing of *Rouletabille chez Krupp*'s. It was the point at which the Germans' Great Spring Offensive was conclusively stopped in March 1918, and the scene of further fierce fighting when the Allies began

Abruptly, he recalled that he had not come to Paris to waste his time in vague philosophical reflections. He hastened his pace toward the newspaper offices, and soon crossed the threshold of *L'Époque*'s great hall.

"Rouletabille! Rouletabille!" With what joy he was still welcomed in that old building, where he had none but comrades! Alas, some had already fallen on the battlefields, and the list of heroic victims was getting longer in the golden book proudly displayed in the hall, in the shadow of Mercié's famous statue, *Gloria Victis!*[8]

Those of an age at which infirmity had retained them in the editorial offices came out to kiss Rouletabille's cheeks or shake his hand. They found him bearing up superbly beneath his muddy carapace. It was quite apt for them to think that "the war had done him good!"

An old servant, however, with a breast bedecked with medals, was already informing the young man that "the boss" was asking for him. The reporter was immediately introduced into the office of the editor-in-chief.

It was not without a certain emotion that Rouletabille went into that room, in which he would certainly learn the perhaps-redoubtable reason for which he had undertaken such an unexpected journey.

The doors had closed again. The boss was alone.

---

to drive the Germans back, retaking the town in August 1918. Georges Clemenceau had uttered his famous quote observing that "les Allemands sont à Noyon" in 1915

[8] A patriotic bronze commemorating the Franco-Prussian War, cast in 1874. Copies of it became commonplace symbols during and after the Great War. The Latin title translates as "Glory to the Vanquished."

The man had always had a great amity for Rouletabille, whom he considered as something akin to a son of the household. Ordinarily, when he saw him again after a long absence or some sensation reportage, he welcomed him joyfully. Why, then, was he silent this time? What was wrong? What had happened? What did this solemnity, to which Rouletabille was not accustomed, signify?

The reported briefly examined his conscience. "Boss, you're frightening me!"

"This isn't the right time to be frightened of anyone or anything, my friend, and when I've told you why you've been ordered to come, you'll share my opinion!"

"You're going to ask me to do something terrible?"

"Yes."

"Speak, Monsieur—I'm listening."

At that moment, the telephone rang, and the director unhooked the apparatus set on his desk.

"Hello? Hello? Oh, very good—it's you, Monsieur le Ministre... Yes, he's here!... In good health, indeed!... No, I haven't said anything to him yet... All he knows is that there's a ninety-nine per cent chance of not coming back from the mission... What did he say? Nothing, of course... Of course he'll accept!... Do I still think so? Of course I think so! He's the only one who can get us out of it... Hello? Hello? It's still on for this evening? Good, good!... Eh? Cromer has arrived from London? Well, what did he say? Hello?... Eh?... Frightful!... Good, good!... Prefect!... Yes, that's much better!... Until this evening!"

The editor hung up the telephone. "You realized that we were talking about you!"

"Which Minister was it?" Rouletabille asked.

"You'll find out this evening—we're meeting him at half past ten."

"Where?"

"At the Ministry of the Interior, where certain other very important people will also be gathering."

"Oh—that means it's a real cabinet meeting."

"Yes, Rouletabille, a real cabinet meeting, but a meeting so secret that it has to remain unknown to all those who aren't taking part in it—a meeting at which you'll learn what's expected of you, my young friend. In the meantime..."

"In the meantime, I'll go take a bath," Rouletabille declared, utterly delighted with the extraordinary complexion of events.

"Go take a bath and come back clean and ready to go. We need all your strength, Rouletabille, all your courage and all your intelligence."

The young man was already at the door, but the voice of his chief had suddenly taken on such a singular weight in pronouncing the last words that he turned round. He saw that the boss was becoming increasing emotional.

"Oh! I've never seen you in such a state, Boss. You're usually so calm! My God, what can this be about?"

The editor took his hands then, leaned toward the reporter and looked into his eyes. "It's quite simply a matter of saving Paris, my young friend. Do you hear, Rouletabille? Saving Paris! Now, until this evening, at half past ten..."

Chapter II
The Secret Cabinet Meeting

The reporter disappeared, escaping down a service stairway. He wanted to be alone; he needed to think.

All in all, he could hardly contain his joy. Since the beginning of the war, he had, like so many others, done his duty obscurely, risking his life a hundred times over in the anonymous needs of national defense, which was certainly full of grandeur, although he would have liked something—let us say the word that was in the back of the reporter's mind—"more amusing." How many times had he not wished that someone might call on his gifts of initiative and invention, in order to carry out some exceptionally difficult mission to which he could have given his entire soul, his entire imagination!

Well, today he had his wish. He had been summoned in order to save Paris! The most important people in the State were looking to Corporal Rouletabille to save Paris! Quite simply!

But what did it mean, though: save Paris?

Those two words were exciting him, dazzling him, although he could not comprehend what form such prodigious adventure might take. He knew full well, having returned from the trenches that *the others* could no longer get through—and everyone else knew that too—and even if they were able to get through, that he could not possibly stop them all on his own! And yet, it followed from the conversation he had just had with his boss that it was him who was going to save Paris—that they were counting on him to save Paris! How, then?

"Some hope!" he said, aloud, on the boulevard that he was in the process of crossing, in order to jump into a cab that would take him to the bath-house...

An hour later, when he came out from there, after some furious hygienic exercise and a solid massage, he found himself much calmer, quite self-composed, ready for any eventuality, all set for any adventure. He dined in a modest restaurant in the Champs-Élysées, in the shade of an arbor, alone with his thoughts and the impatience that he was having difficulty suppressing. He would have liked to show the "very important people" a Rouletabille of marble, whom nothing could disturb.

At ten o'clock he went through the gate of the Place Beauvau. He was immediately shown into the office of the minister's chief aide; the editor of *L'Époque* was already there.

"They're briefing the Minister," the Boss said to him as he shook his hand—and they both stood there, face to face, in silence.

Suddenly, a door opened. An usher showed "the Messieurs" into the Minister's office. A "very important person" was there, whom Rouletabille recognized. Polite formalities were exchanged.

"How goes it with the troops!"

"Fine."

"Sit down then, please.

Another "very important person" arrived, and was introduced to Rouletabille.

"Delighted to meet you, young man. Your editor has told us that impossible things can be asked of you. We shall see..."

Rouletabille did not have time to reply. A third VIP made his entrance. It was the one to whom the editor of

L'Époque had spoken on the telephone as soon as Rouletabille had arrived.

"Well, have you seen Cromer?" everyone asked.

"Cromer," replied the latest arrival, "ought to be upstairs. I told him to meet us at half past ten. What he's revealed is frightful!"

Another door opened, and the head of the Sûreté Générale was announced. "Messieurs," he said, "all my people are here. If you'd care to come up, I'm at your disposal."

So it was to the Sûreté Générale that they were going; they had not wanted to hold the extraordinary meeting in the Ministry itself, but in a more discreet and secluded place.

Through internal stairways and corridors, whose labyrinth Rouletabille knew well, they went to the office of the head of the Sûreté Générale. In the little vestibule preceding the office, a clean-shaven man of Anglo-Saxon appearance, with an energetic expression, was standing with his arms folded, while in the depths of an armchair, an honorable old lady in a black bonnet was displaying a face full of anguish imprinted with infinite sadness. The VIPs bowed to her.

One of them went to the man. "Would you please come in with us, Mr. Cromer."

The old lady had not moved. She remained alone in the vestibule, with the usher, who closed his chief's office door on the others.

In the office, they all sat down.

We have employed a necessary discretion in designating the "very important people" who had been assembled there by the head of the Sûreté Générale, and in order to denote their individuality we shall employ the same terms that Rouletabille used when he had to recall in his notes the role that each one played in the mysterious session.

Firstly, there was the one that everyone addressed as "Monsieur le Président," and sometimes as "Monsieur le Premier," an expression that is used to address the Prime Minister, the President of the Council and also the President of the Parisian Court of Appeal.[9]

The second VIP—the one who had introduced Mr. Cromer—was distinguished by an enormous pair of horn-rimmed spectacles, which set veritable portholes over his clean-shaven face every time he had to read a piece of paper or found it interesting to study the features of his interlocutor. Rouletabille, in referring to him, called him "Horn-rimmed Glasses."[10]

Finally, the third one never stopped smoking enormous cigars, of which he had a profuse supply in a briefcase as large as a small valise. A long time ago, Rouletabille had already nicknamed him "the Tobacconist."[11]

As he went in, the reporter had slipped into a dark corner from which he could see everything, where he hoped to be forgotten.

"Should we send for Nourry?" asked the head of the Sûreté Générale, to begin with.

Horn-rimmed Glasses, bringing some papers out of his morocco portfolio, said: "No, not yet. First I'm going to read you this letter from Fulbert, which the Invention Service has discovered."

---

[9] Presumably Georges Clemenceau, President of the Council and Minister of War.
[10] Probably Stephen Pichon, the Minister of Foreign Affairs
[11] Possibly Louis Loucheur, the Armaments Minister

"You'll admit, my dear friend, that it's quite incredible that the Service could receive such an item!" said the one they called the President.

"The staff of the Service will tell you," Horn-rimmed Glasses replied, "that they receive a hundred of the same sort every month. What's more, they're of all kinds. They ended up finding Fulbert's missive among those that had been rejected as having been written by lunatics!"

With the exception of Rouletabille, everyone there uttered an exclamation, especial the editor of *L'Époque*.

"But Fulbert isn't just anyone!" he said. "His work on the curative virtues of radium were beginning to cause a sensation a few months before the war broke out."

"Bah! Let's not exaggerate," replied Horn-rimmed Glasses. "Let's remember that at that time, the scientific establishment was already beginning to treat Fulbert as a poet and a dreamer. And since you remember the claim he made that all the afflictions of humankind would one day be curable with his radium, imagine the astonishment of the staff of the Inventions on receiving a letter in which the same inventor affirmed that he had found a way of destroying 'in five seconds,' a considerable fraction of that same humankind. Judge for yourselves; I'll read

"To Monsieur etc. etc. I have the honor of informing you that I can put at the disposal of the Office of Inventions the plans for an infernal machine capable of destroying a city the size of Berlin in a few minutes, without leaving our own frontiers. Please believe me, Monsieur le Ministre. Your devoted servant, Théodore Fulbert."

Chapter III
The Tribulations of an Inventor

"Well, you'll admit," said Horn-rimmed Glasses, replacing the singular letter in his portfolio, "that it's quite excusable, after reading such a document, to think that it might emanate from a cracked brain. What do you expect? It might well have been signed Théodore Fulbert, but the tranquil simplicity with which the scientist, who has always been reputed to be rather eccentric, announces to us that he will place himself at our disposal for the destruction of Berlin, would have inclined the least prejudiced individual to offer dire prognostications regarding the imminent future of such a fine intelligence..."

It was then that Mr. Cromer's voice was heard or the first time. That individual spoke French with a very pronounced English accent. He expressed himself with difficulty, but forcefully, and once he had found the term he needed, he launched it at his interlocutor with a brutality that seemed designed to annihilate any trace of dispute or argument.

"Pardon me, Your Excellencies—it's necessary to know that Théodore Fulbert did not even receive any reply. Indeed, that's not saying enough—in my opinion. the poor old scientist has been treated by you like a young man undertaking his first experiments in physics. In my opinion, your inventors are very good, but always regarded as quite mad. Yes, I say so! There are certainly research establishments like the Collège de France and the Museum, but outside of that establishment nothing at all. No! And outside the Pasteur Institute for biological studies, nothing at all for other inventions. No! But in Germany, there is one institute for general research very well endowed with large sums of money, in which the emperor takes a great interest. Yes! In America, in England, generous billionaires have created research institutions—and all your inventors are going to England or America, like Carrel,[12] a Frenchman at the American Rockefeller Institute—and they also went, before the war, to enrich Germany, because patents there are guaranteed by the German government. Yes!"

Beneath this flood of curt phrases, everyone had initially bowed their heads, but, the President having made a gesture of impatience, Horn-rimmed Glasses ventured to interrupt the terrible Mr. Cromer.

"I think it's a little late for us to spend time on these criticisms, perhaps justified..."

"Yes, I'm criticizing. I beg your pardon. That's why I've come. In France, in Paris, as I say, inventors are like children abandoned on the road of science. Théodore Fulbert wrote that to me, and then I read his letter to my Institution personally! I replied! And then he came—and I saw, when I listened to him, how serious and terrible what he was saying was!"

The President interrupted the Englishman again. "Let's proceed in order. Before going to find Mr. Cromer, didn't he communicate with the editor of *L'Époque?*"

"That's right," he latter immediately replied, "and for myself, I did what Mr. Cromer did—I asked Fulbert to come to see me, and I questioned him, and found that

---

[12] The French biologist Alexis Carrel (1873-1944), winner of a Nobel Prize in 1912 for work done in Canada in the early 1900s, joined the Rockefeller Institute in 1906.

everything he had to say was less ridiculous than terrible, as Mr. Cromer says—so terrible that I invited him to dinner that same evening with General D***."

"General D*** is at Salonika,"[13] Horn-rimmed Glasses put in. "I had an opportunity to see him a few days before his departure, He didn't say anything to me about Fulbert..."

"He'd probably forgotten already," said the editor of *L'Époque*.

"Fulbert hadn't made much of an impression on him, then?" asked the Tobacconist.

"All the details of that dinner remain quite clear in my mind," replied the editor of *L'Époque*."

"Please be so kind as to acquaint us with them, Monsieur!" said the President.

"Well, that evening, over the soup, Fulbert—without revealing his secret, naturally—told us about the formidable power of his device, and I recall that he hadn't been talking for five minutes when General D*** exclaimed: 'But this is a Jules Verne story you're telling us, my dear scientist. I read it when I was at school, it's called *Les Cinq cents millions de la Begum!*[14] Hang on, this is the subject, which I remember quite clearly: a Boche of those days had built a prodigious cannon that projected a colossal projectile, capable of annihilating

---

[13] Maurice Sarrail was the French commander of the Allied armies on the Macedonian Front in Salonika in the early months of 1917; the novel was serialized before his replacement in November, but "General D***" is more likely to be Henry Descoin, commander of the garrison at Korçë in Albania.

[14] Based on a manuscript by Paschal Grousset (alias André Laurie), this novel, known in English as *The Begum's Fortune*, was first published in 1879.

everything in a matter of minutes, at a city built in America by Frenchmen!'

"In order to say that, General D*** had adopted a tone so utterly sarcastic that I thought I ought to intervene. 'My dear general,' I interjected, 'we're living in a era in which all the imaginations of Jules Verne, on land, in the air and under the sea, are being realized so well and so completely that it's unnecessary to be astonished by this one entering the domain of reality like all the rest.'

"When I said that, Fulbert, who was sitting across from us, fixed the general and myself with an expression of immeasurable scorn. 'Imaginative as Jules Verne was,' he exclaimed, 'he never dared to dream of what present-day science is capable of materializing. In my own case, it's not a matter of a shell but a torpedo[15]— and a torpedo that no cannon in the world could contain and no charge of any known explosive could propel very far! My torpedo is bigger than the *Titanic*! Bigger than the *Titanic*, do you hear? It's three hundred meters long. It's capable of a speed of four hundred kilometers an hour. Nothing can stop it! It ruins everything, burns everything and annihilates everything within a radius of several leagues. Nothing can prevail against it once it is launched. Nothing is capable of preventing it from hitting its target squarely, or of exploding at a determined time in a determined location. Its name is *Titania*.'

---

[15] The French term *torpille* [torpedo] had a wider range of reference at this time that it acquired when the term was largely restricted to water-borne missiles fired by submarines; it could be used to refer to any kind of "guided missile." I have refrained from substituting the latter term because its use would be anachronistic.

"I don't know whether you have ever seen Théodore Fulbert," the editor of *L'Époque* continued. "He has eyes of a child-like brightness and purity, the face of a small inspired angel, within an untidy frame of white tresses, which twist like flames around his phenomenal forehead—and the whole constitutes a curious mixture that's astonishing and disturbing.

"That evening, he was very, very disturbing. When he got up from the table, having launched his formidable tirade at us, he seemed literally crazy…and I wouldn't have been surprised if he'd fallen down in front of us with an attack of apoplexy.

"It was as if he forgot to shake my hand and didn't notice that it was in my automobile that I had him taken home. When he'd gone, General D said to me: 'He's not the first man the war has driven mad. No matter! We've had in interesting evening! He's amusing, with his torpedo!' Then we talked about something else.

"The next day, I received a note from Fulbert telling me that he had decided to offer his infernal machine to the English and asking whether I could facilitate his journey and obtain the necessary permits for him. I took care of it immediately, simply in order not to annoy him—and that's how he came to cross the Channel. He'd already written to Mr. Cromer at the Scarborough Institute—and I soon learned the Mr. Cromer had taken seriously that which had simply amused General D*** and myself."

Having said that, the editor of *L'Époque* fell silent, and everyone in the office of the head of the Sûreté Générale looked at Mr. Cromer—and there was certainly a certain emotions in that group of "very important people" when the Englishman was heard to say:

"Very good! Théodore Fulbert is not mad at all. I say, yes, he could destroy Berlin!"

Chapter IV
A Giant Torpedo

After a brief silence, the President leaned toward Mr. Cromer and said: "Mr. Cromer, I'd like to know whether the opinion you've just offered relative to the interesting invention of Théodore Fulbert is the result of experiments that have been carried out before your eyes?"

"Of course—the direct result."

"And Fulbert hasn't exaggerated the incredible power of his device?"

"No—no exaggeration."

"That's entirely affirmative! Mr. Cromer, we shall envisage the whole truth with courage. Can you tell us how you arrived, on your own account, at such a clear, and also redoubtable, conclusion?"

"There are things that I can say about the machine and things that I can't."

"Then tell us what you can say, Mr. Cromer."

"All right. To begin with, I can say that I received Théodore Fulbert with the respect that one owes to an unfortunate old scientist who had distinguished himself so much with regard to the medicinal properties of radium. And immediately, when he told me that he had invented a machine to destroy Berlin, I said that that was not in his medical field—and he replied that it *was* in his medical field, because, in destroying Berlin, his machine would be destroying a disease of the earth!"

In spite of the difficulty that Mr. Cromer was having in expressing himself and the effort that his listeners had to make to follow his narration, the latter was so interesting that there was no room for an interruption, or even a smile.

Mr. Cromer related that Fulbert had brought his plans to him. After two days of explanations, Cromer had been convinced. He had was not in possession of the final secret that ensured the mathematical functioning of the formidable apparatus, but Fulbert had not hesitated to confide to an ally of Cromer's scientific and moral value the principle of the secret of the new explosive with which his torpedo was loaded, and which also served for its propulsion.

In sum, the novelty of the disposition of the turbines, the helices of suspension and those of direction, and a certain rudder counterbalancing the ailerons, whose function was to bring the engine back automatically to the hypothetical line traced between its point of departure and point of arrival, in spite of any possible perturbations of the atmosphere—all those technical details—had amply proved to Cromer, from the start, that he was facing an endeavor matured for a long time by a man to whom none of the problems of the new aviation and ballistics were unfamiliar.

Cromer had therefore been seduced from the very beginning by the terrible *Titania*, of which no one in France had wanted to hear mention.

Here, Cromer judged it necessary to explain the intentions that were henceforth his in their entirety.

"I ought to say immediately, Your Excellencies, and you, Messieurs, that I never had it in mind to destroy Berlin, for we are not savages, but I did want to discover whether, instead of that machine, which would have cost at least sixty million, one might be able to make small *Titanias*, less expensive and designed specifically to destroy citadels and forts at long range and in a sure fashion, without risking the life of a single Tommy. But I did not confide my intention to Fulbert, who was absolutely determined to destroy Berlin in order to terrify Germany and bring a sudden end to war throughout the world.

"In conversation, Théodore had been absolutely fervent about his fabrication of sixty-million-franc *Titania*—but as you can imagine, that was not my dream at all. So I told him that it would first be necessary to construct a scale model, a little *Titania* twenty-five meters long, and asked him how expensive that would be. He replied that he thought that it would cost at least five million francs. Then I spoke to the Privy Council of my Institute. In spite of everything I could say, they said that it was too dear for something problematic.

"Then I went to London and brought back a very rich English patriot, who doesn't want his name to be known, and who was also very interested, and said he would provide all the money required.

"Fulbert didn't want any money for himself or his family, but he wept with joy at the idea that he was going to work on the little *Titania* while waiting for the big one."

After that, Cromer related how, in three months, piece by piece, the little *Titania* was constructed in various workshops, and how the pieces were eventually brought together for assembly in a secret institution built for that purpose at the northern tip of the Isle of Man, in the middle of the Irish Sea, on land belonging to the wealthy English patriot. There, a special team from the Scarborough Institute worked under Fulbert's direction and Cromer's supervision.

The inventor had brought his wife and his daughter Nicole, as well as his daughter's fiancé, a Pole who had been collaborating in the father's work for five years, and had particular responsibility for the manufacture of the explosive.

"This is what I can tell you about the explosive," Cromer specified. "It's a liquid air explosive, admirable for both explosion and propulsion." And he gave a few details, reticently. He was evidently conscious that he had a crowd of unfamiliar ears around him. Several times, he darted suspicious glances at the dark corner in which Rouletabille had tucked himself away.

He explained in a rather embarrassed and perhaps deliberately confused fashion that the economical industrial manufacture of liquid air now permitted oxygen to be obtained in a simple form to serve for the combustion of explosive mixtures. Fulbert had personally discovered a procedure permitting him to use liquid oxygen directly, in very particular conditions related to the fabrication of oxylignite.[16] It is well-known that one obtains oxylignite, patented in Germany in 1898, by steeping a cartridge containing either charcoal, pulverized cork, fossil Kieselguhr impregnated with petroleum or black powder in liquid air for a few minutes. Fulbert added a new element to a cartridge containing pulverized cork, for which he did not have a patent, but whose secret he had confided in good faith to Cromer.

From all that resulted a blast incomparably more powerful than that of melinite of Boche TNT, but above all of an asphyxiating and incendiary power astonishing in such a small volume. The only inconveniences of the

---

[16] The use of liquid oxygen as an explosive was relatively short-lived, but cartridges intended for that purpose were manufactured for some years at the Linde factory in Munich under the name of oxylignite.

mixture were that of being extremely inflammable, and that of losing most of its force of any circumstance permitted the liquid air to evaporate. There was nothing of that kind to fear with regard to the *Titania*, which the genius of Fulbert had made into a "marvel"—to make use of Cromer's enthusiastic expression.

"It's the marvel of marvels," he exclaimed. "Even more so than the explosive, in fact, and I can say right way what a great marvel the big *Titania* will be. You know how a Zeppelin can carry little balloons in its belly; well, the big *Titania* conceals forty little *Titanias* in its entrails. Actually, I should say forty little things like little torpedoes. And when he big *Titania* explodes at its destination, those little *Titanias*, carried by precisely-regulated clockwork mechanisms, disperse around the center and explode in their turn at points determined in such a fashion that an entire circle several leagues in diameter is covered in ruins...and corpses. Yes, full of corpses! Put a city within that circle, and one or two million inhabitants in that city, and an hour after the arrival of the *Titania*, there would be none at all. What admirable work!"

Another silence, even more marked than the others followed Cromer's last words. Then the Tobacconist, who had let his cigar go out—which testified to the enormity of his emotion—asked for a light and a few explanations.

"In my opinions, I think Mr. Cromer has assumed a great deal on the basis of the small experiment he has carried out, regarding the complete success of such a vast experiment as the Titania imagined by Fulbert, whose realization would inevitably encounter difficulties and perhaps impossibilities..."

"No, Your Excellency, no! Not impossibilities! It's perfectly possible! Yes—the little *Titania* was constructed exactly as the large one would be, with little torpedoes inside it, loaded with Fulbert explosive and directed by exactly the same mechanism. I can tell you this: the interior of the *Titania* is divided into three sections; much the largest is t contain the forty torpedoes loaded with explosive; the second section is occupied by the propulsive charge; and the third by all the machinery, which is very complicated and methodical. As for the disposition of the helices of suspension and turbines of propulsion, everything works perfectly. But the exact secret of the impossibility of changing direction and the perfect automatic intelligence of the engine in reverting to its direct route, in spite of the most terrible storm and perturbation, I shall never disclose because I shall never know it. Théodore Fulbert has taken that secret with him, alas. What a pity!"

Horn-rimmed Glasses then took the floor: "Mr. Cromer, I have told these Messieurs briefly the extraordinary results of the experiment that took place before your eyes, but it would be useful to hear the details from your own mouth."

Cromer nodded his head, and then recounted that when the torpedo had been completed in the workshops in the Isle of Man, Fulbert, aided by his Polish assistant, had, at the last minute, introduced into the machine the box enclosing the mysterious mechanism that connected the compensating rudder to the ailerons. Then the signal for the torpedo's departure had been given by the man who had provided the funds for the costly experiment.

The rich Englishman had acquired, for the occasion, a small island situated about two hundred kilometers to the north-north-west of the Isle of Man, off Cape Fair.[17]

Before arriving at its destination, which was that small island, the torpedo had to pass over the peninsula that terminates the southern Highlands to the west. The admiralty had been warned and all precautions taken, at sea as on land.

The small island contained a village and three hamlets of fishermen, who had been evacuated, but fifty cattle and three hundred sheep were disembarked.

Immediately after the departure of the torpedo, which left its tube with no other noise than a furious hiss, the Pole, Mademoiselle Fulbert, Cromer, the rich Englishman and a delegate from the War Office embarked in an automatic launch. They soon heard the distant echo of the explosion, which must have been formidable. When they arrived within sight of the island where the explosion had taken place, about an hour and a half later, nothing remained but embers.

They were obliged to wait a further two hours before they could land, because of the asphyxiating gases, heavy clouds of which pursued them even over the waters. Finally, when they set foot on the ground, they were left in no doubt as to the extent of the disaster. There was absolutely nothing left on the island, thriving only a few minutes before. The villages, the woods, the cattle and the sheep had all been reduced to ashes; everything was dead. They were walking over an immense black rock.

---

[17] There is no such Cape; Leroux might be thinking about Cape Wrath, much further to the north, although the distance he gives is more suggestive of Iona, of the island of Mull.

Confronted by this terrible result, Théodore Fulbert had rubbed his hands. "How do you expect anything to resist me thermite?" he said. "It explodes at a temperature of ten thousand degrees. With my thermite and my *Titania*, it's the end of war!" And the old man had started dancing with you like a child, over the smoking ruins that he had made.

In order to describe the Dantean aspect that the piece of land sacrificed to the genius of destruction had offered to him, Cromer had found terms so evocative in their harshness that his auditors could not help feeling once again the frisson that corresponded to an idea they already had, but that Rouletabille had not yet succeeded in specifying. In fact, he could not yet see anything in all of this that threatened Paris.

The reporter was soon to be enlightened.

The next few sentences pronounced, with a particular emotion, by Cromer finally put Rouletabille on the redoubtable track on which he might perhaps leave his intelligence and his bones.

"The very evening of that terrible explosion, we all returned to the Isle of Man—well content, in truth. We had dinner, and toasted the success of the experiment with champagne. The next day, however, Théodore Fulbert did not meet me, as arranged, at the workshop. I thought that the poor man had a hangover from the champagne, so I went to his cottage on the Isle of Man. I found his wife unconscious and tied to the bed, her mouth gagged with a handkerchief—but I didn't find Fulbert or Mademoiselle Fulbert, and I didn't find the Polish fiancé either! And in Fulbert's study I could no longer find the original plans of the *Titania* or any of Fulbert's own papers. Everything had been taken, removed during the night—and an investigation immediately revealed that the Boche had been there, and had abducted the three people and taken away all the plans and papers in a boat that had returned to a submarine.

"The government was immediately alerted. The Admiralty gave its orders: a hundred destroyers started hunting for the submarine, but without any result.

"We had been robbed, stupidly. Yes—it's terrible!"

Chapter V
Madame Fulbert

Horn-rimmed Glasses, the Tobacconist, the Boss and the head of the Sûreté Générale were agitated. The President lit a cigarette from the Tobacconist's cigar, blew out the smoke, gazed at it momentarily rising in blue spirals toward the ceiling, and said: "And now it's against us that this frightful experiment has turned."

"Do we really have anything to fear?" asked the Tobacconist, hesitantly.

"Do we have anything to fear!" exclaimed Horn-rimmed Glasses. "You'll see, my dear colleague, when you've heard Nourry!"

"Should I bring Nourry in?" asked the head of the Sûreté Générale.

"No," replied the President. "First, have Madame Fulbert come in."

Everyone got up when Madame Fulbert entered the room.

The President addressed a few comforting words to her, confirming the news that had already been communicated to him, that her husband and daughter were prisoners in Germany but in good health, apparently in no danger, and that it was necessary, in consequence, not to despair of seeing them emerge soon from that frightful adventure. After which Madame Fulbert was invited to sit down.

She sat down, shaking her head sadly. She was the old lady that Rouletabille had noticed in the vestibule.

Her face was strained and distressed, and all the sadness that had spread within her seemed as old as she was.

"Can you, Madame," asked the President, "give us some details regarding the circumstances in which the abduction of your husband and daughter took place.?"

"I've already answered that question," the old lady said, in a vice as soft as that of a little girl. "I didn't see or hear anything. What more can I add? I was tied up and gagged in darkness, and fainted in terror."

"During the evening, did the Pole remain with you all the time? Did he go home with you? Did he go to bed at the same time as you?"

"I have every reason to think so, Monsieur. He wished us all good night, and shut himself in his room."

"You didn't suspect anything? You all went to sleep full of hope?"

"Full of hope!" interjected the old lady. "Speaking for myself, I had no longer had any for a long time. My husband has never been happy about anything. Everything he has attempted has always turned against him—against us. This will end the same way. His inventions have ruined us and caused us countless troubles. My daughter's dowry, like mine, has melted away in the crucible of his costly experiments. However, neither I nor my daughter ever complained. We loved that man as God has made him."

"Was not your daughter the fiancée of Monsieur Fulbert's assistant?" the President asked.

"Yes, Monsieur, and that too was a misfortune in my eyes. I knew that I had suffered with an inventor and I would have liked my daughter to enjoy another existence than the one made for me—but I confessed myself vanquished right away. Nicole is twenty-five years old.

She's very pretty but she hasn't a sou. Then again, she loves her Pole."

"Can you give us a few details regarding Monsieur Fulbert's assistant?" asked Horn-rimmed Glasses then. "In the present circumstances, they might be precious to us. We don't want to surprise you. The first idea that occurred to us was that in the business of the abduction and the theft of the *Titania*'s plans, that foreigner might have done you a disservice..."

"I don't think so, Messieurs," the old lady replied, without raising her voice. No, I really don't think so. I'd put my hand in the fire to swear that Serge Rejitsky is incapable of betraying us."

"However, if he had wanted to, he would have been able to do it, wouldn't he?"

"Certainly! He was party to all my husband's secrets and speculations, to which he added his own."

"There was nothing he did not know about the most secret mechanism of the *Titania*?"

"Nothing, Monsieur."

"Even though your husband had judged it prudent not to reveal it to Mr. Cromer, his assistant knew it?"

"Yes, Monsieur, he knew everything."

"That's categorical," observed Horn-rimmed Glasses to the other VIPs. "The Pole knew everything, and he can do everything."

There was a pause, and then the President resumed: "In order for you to affirm, Madame, in such a clear fashion, that the man is incapable of abusing the secrets he possesses, you must undoubtedly believe that he is entirely devoted to France, or at least to the Allies' cause?"

"No, Monsieur no—it's not for any patriotic reason that I believe him to be incapable of infamy. If I've said

44

that, it's because I know his character and his love for my daughter."

At this point the head of the Sûreté Générale asked for permission to ask a question.

"Did you know, Madame, that Serge Rejitsky is not the real name of Mademoiselle Fulbert's fiancé?"

"We knew that, Monsieur. His real name is Serge Kaniewsky, and under that name he has been pursued in Poland and in Russia, and arrested in France and put on trial with a group of anarchists. He was sentenced to five years in prison, even though nothing precise was proven against him."

"In brief," the head of the Sûreté Générale put in, "he's a man who has suffered a great deal, and who believes that he has been unjustly condemned by France. He's a man who can't have any great love for France."

"That's possible, Monsieur, but my daughter loves France, and you can be sure that her Serge will act as if he felt the same, for in that respect, Serge knows full well that my daughter would not forgive him for any weakness, let alone treason. For Serge, I repeat, there is no longer anyone in the world but my daughter. He arrived in our home, dying of hunger, proscribed by all the police forces on earth, with formidable ideas of vengeance against the human race—the man had never known anything but hatred. He was ugly, morally and physically. Physically, you hear, Messieurs—very ugly rather than simply ugly. It was sufficient for my daughter to lean over that wreck...and another man was born. Now, Serge knows that he is loved, for my daughter loves him, because of his fiery soul, akin to her own. Now, Serge knows love! The rest—the past, he present, the future, outside of that love—no longer exists. He would blow up the world for a smile from my daughter; he would

45

refrain from killing a fly in order not to give her grief. You can be tranquil, Messieurs, quite tranquil..."

And the benevolent old lady, shaking her head, seemed to want to reassure everyone.

The gentlemen thanked her, and addressed a few more kind words to her. The head of the Sûreté Générale escorted her as far as the vestibule.

When he came back, the gentlemen were all in agreement in proclaiming that, far from tranquilizing them, what the old lady had said had increased their anxiety considerably.

"My opinion," declared the editor of *L'Époque*, squarely, "is that we now have everything to fear!"

"In any case," said Horn-rimmed Glasses, "we ought to act as if we had everything to fear."

"And act without losing a minute!" added the Tobacconist.

"Have Nourry come in!" ordered the President.

Immediately, silence was reestablished. The head of the Sûreté Générale opened a door that connected with a small private room, and a man was shown in.

Chapter VI
Nourry

He was still young, with a very intelligent face, and seemed to have suffered a great deal physically. He had an arm in a sling. He was dressed in the rather unorthodox costume of a convalescent *poilu*. He was invited to sit down.

The head of the Sûreté Générale said to him: "Nourry, you're going to tell us everything that happened to you in Essen since the day when you met Malet, and then how you both escaped, and how Malet was killed at the Dutch frontier."

The mean began immediately. "Messieurs, I was taken prisoner at Yser. I was immediately taken to the camp at Rastatt. I had only been there a week when I was asked whether I might like to work in my profession at Essen, for Krupp's.

"I'm a graduate of the École des Arts et Métiers. For five years I was at the head of a major cutlery business in Guéret. The Boche had learned these details from my papers. I replied to them: 'If it's to manufacture bayonets or work on munitions, there's nothing doing.' They said to me: 'No, it's to make scissors, women's scissors for sewing.' I thought they were having me on, but I said to myself: *it's always as well to take a look*, and I replied: 'Okay!'

"And I arrived in Essen. As well as the factories, there are prisoner-of-war camps there. The majority of the prisoners had simply been requisitioned to work on the roads, but there were a few hundred who were taken out of the camp into the morning to work in the factories, from which they were brought back in the evening. They weren't required to work on munitions. It's an error to believe, as I'd believed for a long time myself, that the factories at Essen only make cannon, shells, armor and other war materials; in fact, a fairly large section of the workshops produces articles of very various sorts, intended to be exchanged for foodstuffs or other basic necessities n neutral countries.

"I've seen products made at Essen heaped up on the docks of the Ruhr, at Duisburg—machines and machine components-that were about to leave for Sweden, sent there in exchange for oil, fish, paper and wood. The Krupp factories send knives, scissors, sewing-machines and utensils of every sort to Holland. In particular, al the French prisoners who had been employed before the war in manufacturing sewing-machines are sure of receiving an offer to work at Essen. If they accept, they're treated well, and even receive a reasonable wage. If they refused, they're only making things more miserable for themselves.

"It wasn't in the workshops that I met Malet but in the camp, one evening, while having a glass of beer in the canteen. He wasn't working in the steel mill, but in the radiology section. For months, he'd been employed in the manufacture of military radiological vehicles; that was his specialty. When they found out that he'd worked before the war in Professor Laval's laboratory at the Sorbonne, they sent him to the Energy Laboratory which the chief engineer of inventions had recently created in the huge Research Center.

"More than once, Malet told me that, in his opinion, it wasn't always with the objective of healing injuries that certain experiments with radium were being carried out in the Energy Laboratory. At any rate, it was there that Malet was surprised to see, one day, a familiar face: that of the inventor Théodore Fulbert. What was he doing there? How had he come to be taken prisoner? Malet asked himself that for some time without being able to find an answer.

"Fulbert was closely watched. He only went through the laboratory to be locked up in a small workroom specially reserved for him—but one day, Fulbert spotted Malet and recognized him. He made him a sign indicating that he needed to speak to him. A week later I saw Malet arrive in the canteen very pale, quite incapable of hiding his emotion. 'Let's take a walk,' he said to me—and he led me very gently, without seeming to be doing anything in particular, to the Kullmann bakery situated in the north-western corner of the camp. We were served coffee and liqueurs there, clandestinely, in the back room. Frau Kullmann let us in there quite often, because we paid well for those few minutes of solitude. Indeed, she closed the door on us, and that was the only moment of the day when the Boche could no longer see us. It was much appreciated.

"The back room had a window with overlooked the northern section of the factories. For some time, through that window, we had seen an enormous wooden building being constructed on the causeway inside the surrounding wall, whose length we couldn't even measure, because it was hidden from us by other buildings and the accumulation of temporary shops that had been constructed since the war.

"The building had the peculiarity that it wasn't constructed in alignment with the others, nor parallel to them; it was orientated obliquely, north-east to south-west, as if positioned across, and cutting through, all the rest—and because of that, a number of workshops had been demolished.

"If it hadn't been absurd to imagine that such an impracticable location had been chosen for landing dirigibles, we might have been able to believe that they were in the process of constructing some sort of Zeppelin hangar. In the same way, had the building been erected on the sea shore, we could have believed that it was to serve for the construction of the largest ship in the world. Malet and I had, therefore, been very intrigued by the vision of that fantastic edifice, all the more bizarre because its roof was much higher at the southern end than the northern end.

"That day, as soon as we were alone in the back room of the bakery, Malet drew me to the window, pointed to the gigantic framework and said: 'Everything we've imagined is short of the truth. Do you know what they're going to build in there? An almighty torpedo designed to reduce Paris to ashes in a matter of minutes!'

"I couldn't help shrugging my shoulders at first, so far did the project seem to surpass the limits of human possibility—but Malet wasn't a child. He was, moreover, a scientist; and as he spoke, I was attained in my turn by the most somber fear...

"He told me that he had managed, without being seen, to get into Fulbert's private workroom for a few minutes. It was there that the inventor had told him about the terrible adventure that had undergone.

He and his daughter, and his daughter's fiancé, the Pole Serge Kaniewsky, of whom there was so much talk during the trial of the anarchists, had been taken prisoner by the Boche on the English coast while all three of them were in the process of carrying out trials, on a reduced scale, of a prodigious machine capable of destroying a city at an enormous distance. At the same time as they had abducted the inventors and taken them aboard a submarine, the well-informed Boche had also stolen all the plans and papers related to the invention.

"The captives, brought to Essen, had been put to work constructing, on behalf of Germany, the aerial torpedo they had intended to use against it. In fact, the Boche could do nothing without the cooperation of the inventors, because the plans they possessed only contained diagrams of the general disposition of the machinery, while the principal secret of the invention and certain key figures were only known to Fulbert and Kaniewsky, and had never been written down.

"The two men had declared that no one would get anything out of them, and protested against the unjustifiable violence that had been one to them. In order o put an end to their resistance, the Boche had not hesitated to torture Fulbert's daughter, Mademoiselle Nicole. They had begun by depriving her of any food. When the Pole had seen his fiancée reduced to a state of near-death, he had been unable to endure the spectacle and had promised to do everything that was asked of him. Kaniewsky had therefore given up the chemical formula of the explosive and the secret of the machinery, but had given false figures for the latter. The Boche had set to work immediately. They had recognized the exactitude of the chemical formula and did not suspect that the Pole, who had also been promised a fortune, had not told the whole truth.

"Fulbert forgave Kaniewsky for having given up the formula of his liquid air explosive, for it had been observed that, at Essen itself, Germany was working on a new TNT that was not far from having all the qualities of his thermite. That was not the danger. What Fulbert feared, above all else, was the moment when the Boche discovered that Kaniewsky had deceived them in regard to the secret machinery of the torpedo—which was bound to happen in four or five months' time.

"Obviously, Kaniewsky had wanted to gain time. Perhaps he had hoped that during those five months the war might end, or at least that some fortunate event might save the captives from the desperate situation in which they found themselves. But what Fulbert knew was that Kaniewsky was incapable of seeing Nicole suffer. That, Malet told me, was the reason for the inventor's incessant torment, which prevented him from sleeping and gave him the appearance of a madman.

"'Every minute that goes by,' Fulbert had croaked, 'brings us nearer to the fatal deadline! An imprudence on Kaniewsky's part could precipitate matters. Kaniewsky's determination is not reliable, since he knows that Nicole might die. Mine also totters at that idea, but so far as I'm concerned, I'm sure that I can resist; not one word will pass my lips, not a single figure emerge from my pen, whereas, with Kaniewsky, anything might happen. He might do anything, and they know how to get it out of him. It's necessary to remember that the man lived for years with the sole idea of the ruination and destruction of the world. It's necessary not to forget that Paris has treated him cruelly as Moscow or St. Petersburg, and that he only escaped the dungeons of Schlusselburg to find the cells of the Conciergerie. In sum, he's a man who would sacrifice the human race without hesitation to spare my daughter a minor injury.'

"That day, Malet also told me that Fulbert and Kaniewsky had been kept completely apart, the latter having been installed at the center of the works that had been immediately begun for the construction of the machine. The inventor had also been separated from his daughter. Apart from that he had been treated well and permitted to continue his studies of the curative powers of radium—for the Boche are not barbarians.

"While Malet was telling me these things, I could not take my eyes off that frightful building, from the framework of which a whole population of workers was suspended, and which would soon hide the preparations for the greatest crime in the world—and I trembled with horror, for I no longer doubted it. The Boche are too practical to built such a colossus on the basis of a chimera. Malet and I shook hands feverishly. We had the same thought. 'Old man,' I said, 'there's only one thing to do—we need to get out of here and warn them, back home. There are two of us; one can surely get through.'

"At that very moment, our escape was decided.

"Malet did not see Fulbert again. Had someone seen something, or did someone suspect that he had talked to Fulbert? Did they fear that he might communicate with him again? At any rate, Malet was not take back into the workshop, and was sent to the military radiology unit that had been set up near the city. That circumstance worked to our advantage. I won't bother to recount the details of the escape plan that we prepared carefully for three weeks.

"One night, with a certain amount of luck, we got through the double cordon of sentries, but the following morning we were faced with insurmountable difficulties. The alarm had been raised very rapidly and they were searching for us everywhere, with unparalleled determination. For a fortnight, it was impossible for us to leave the hiding-place that we had reached by swimming, under an old bridge on the Ruhrort, not far from the confluence of the Ruhr and the Rhine.

"When we got under way again, we had exhausted our provisions six days earlier, and we were dying of hunger. Malet, especially, was at the end of his tether. He begged me to abandon him, but I couldn't resolve myself to do that, in spite of everything he could say.

"Finally, just as we were about to cross the Dutch frontier on a pitch-dark night, gunshots rang out behind us. My companion fell at my feet, while I was wounded in the arm. 'Save yourself,' Malet shouted to me, 'and remember!' They were his last words.

"I saved myself, Monsieur, and I've remembered as much as possible. I've often thought about the conversations I had with Malet about Fulbert's revelations, and I think I've repeated in a sufficiently precise fashion the words that he heard from the inventor's mouth."

Nourry had concluded his long narration. It had been heard in the most religious and most anxious silence. They continued to listen when he had fallen silent.

Suddenly, a voice that had not yet been heard emerged from the darkest corner.

"Forgive me, Monsieur, but can you tell me whether the sewing-machines that are being manufactured at Essen are equipped for chain-stitching with one thread or two?"

Astonished by the question, as was everyone else, Nourry replied: "They're of all kinds, Monsieur. Machines for chain-stitching with one thread, machines for overstitching, machines for lock-stitching with two threads, machines for double chain-stitching with two threads, machines for stitching footwear, etc."

"Thank you, Monsieur—that's all I wanted to know."

"You don't have any other questions to ask Monsieur Nourry?" asked the head of the Sûreté Générale, who could not help smiling at the reporter in spite of the gravity of the circumstances.

"None," replied Rouletabille, with the utmost seriousness. And as he had moved slightly forward, he retreated into the shadows.

The Ministers congratulated Nourry appropriately, instructed him to maintain the utmost discretion, and then let him go. The head of the Sûreté accompanied him.

Chapter VII
Rouletabille's Idea

As soon as the door had closed again, the gentlemen rose to their feet and all began talking at the same time, with the exception of the President, who seemed very anxious, plunged into reflections so profound that he did not notice that his cigarette was singeing his moustache.

Cromer was not the least agitated, giving the lie to the traditional reputation of British phlegm—but in this case, it was excusable, for, having already seen the machine in action, he had more reason than anyone else to judge it redoubtable. He stretched his long arms, folded them, unfolded them again, put his hands together, cracked his knuckles, and said: "Now that you're convinced, what are you going to do? Are you going to try to destroy the *Titania* by sending aircraft to drop bombs on it?"

Immediately, all gazes turned to Horn-rimmed Glasses, and Horn-rimmed Glasses said: "Undoubtedly, we can always try that, but apart from the fact that it's far from a sure means, it wouldn't prevent the Germans from reconstructing a similar machine, in such a fashion as to shield it from any further attack of that sort."

"It would delay things while we find something better," opined the Tobacconist, throwing away his cigar, which he had not been smoking for some time.

"That's true," agreed the President, also getting rid of the butt of his incendiary cigarette. "That's true. We need to find something else. Something extraordinary, but on which, nevertheless, we can rely completely—

something that will rid us of any such menace forever. Think of it, Messieurs—if they can destroy Paris, what can the Germans not demand of us in return for not destroying it?"

"Of course! That's frightful! Frightful!"

The editor of *L'Époque* had not yet said anything since Nourry's departure. He had been content to glance from time to time in the direction of the shadow in which Rouletabille had buried himself, but, as the reporter had not yet budged, he ended up by uttering a few words in an impatient tone.

"Well, what do you think, Rouletabille?"

"Yes, may we know what Monsieur Rouletabille thinks?" asked Horn-rimmed Glasses, turning abruptly toward the young man. "For, after all," he added, "if we bought you here, it's because your editor told us that you're acquainted with Essen."

"Oh, I've only passed through it! I undertook the journey to interview Bertha Krupp—a rapid and futile expedition, because Bertha Krupp, on the emperor's orders, refused to see me."[18]

"You nevertheless came back with an article that was reprinted throughout the world, and is perhaps the

_____

[18] Bertha Krupp, the elder child and heir of Friedrich Alfred Krupp, was the sole proprietor of the Krupp industrial empire from 1902-1943, although her husband Gustav von Bohlen und Halbach actually ran the company; their marriage was arranged by Kaiser Wilhelm II because a woman was considered incapable of running the concern, and Gustav added Krupp to his surname to complete his qualifications. It was in Bertha Krupp's "honor" that the Allied troops nicknamed German long-range artillery pieces "Big Berthas" (she was not a slim woman).

most amusing of all those you've written," the editor of *L'Époque* declared.

"Indeed!" agreed the Tobacconist. "I remember it very well. The article was entitled 'How I failed to see Bertha Krupp.'"

"Yes, I failed, completely—and I congratulate myself for it all the more today," said Rouletabille.

"Oh, really?" said Horn-rimmed Glasses. "You congratulate yourself for that today? Have you an idea, then, Monsieur Rouletabille?"

"Rouletabille always has ideas," affirmed the editor of *L'Époque*.

"Yes," the reporter replied, "I have an idea, but I don't know whether it will be agreeable to you, for I heard just now that an extraordinary idea was required, and mine is the most ordinary in the world."

"Let's hear your ordinary idea, then, young man," said the Tobacconist.

"Well, I have the idea of going to Essen and enabling Théodore Fulbert, his daughter and his daughter's fiancé to escape—for they certainly won't agree to go if all three can't go together—and to do that, of course, before the Boche are in possession of the secret of the *Titania*."

"And you think that's an ordinary idea, do you?" said Horn-rimmed Glasses, in amazement.

"It's an idea so ordinary, Monsieur, that it can't fail."

"But if it does fail, what will you do?"

"Why, Monsieur, the only thing left for me to do, and which is indicated to me in a precise fashion by rational deduction. If I can't save the three people who possess the secret of the *Titania*, I shall have no option, in order to preserve the secret in an absolutely secure fashion, as Monsieur demands, but to kill all three of them."

This had been said in a voice so clear and trenchant that everyone there took a step toward the young reporter with a unanimous movement, under the impulse of the same emotion.

However, although they did not doubt for a second that Rouletabille was capable of doing what he said, if the opportunity presented itself, they did not take long to conclude that there was every chance that opportunity would not present itself, and that it would be almost impossible to give rise to it. Was it not necessary first to get to Essen?

"And then, I can't see how you're going to be able, on your own..." said the President.

"That's his business! That's his business!" said the editor of *L'Époque*. "When Rouletabille says something..."

"To begin with," Rouletabille put it, "I didn't say that I'd handle the matter on my own..."

"I warn you," declared Horn-rimmed Glasses, smiling, "that I don't have many men to spare, and that that you shouldn't ask me for an army to capture Essen!"

"Rouletabille has no need of an army," declared the editor of *L'Époque*. "With two of his comrades he sustained a siege for a week in an old tower at Istrandja-Dahg, against three thousand Pomaks with cannon."[19]

"Messieurs," said the reporter, "if the two comrades that the Boss has just mentioned consent to accompany and assist me, I swear to you that there's a ninety-nine per cent chance that my plan will succeed."

---

[19] As related in *Rouletabille à la guerre*.

"In the old days, Rouletabille," growled the editor, "You'd have set off alone, and you wouldn't have granted a one per cent chance of the failure of your project. You would simply have said: 'I'm off, and I'll succeed.'"

"Yes, but in the old days, I wasn't dealing with the Boche," the reporter replied.

At that moment, a door opened abruptly and the distressed face of the head of the Sûreté reappeared. He seemed to be prey to a quite extraordinary emotion—and must, indeed have been, for the chief was renowned for his composure, which never abandoned him, even in the most difficult circumstances.

"Messieurs! Messieurs!" the man stammered, in a fearful voice. "As I was leaving, Nourry—whom I'd arranged to meet tomorrow—was accosted by two drunkards at the corner of the Rue de Saussaies. Nourry called for help, but the agents arrived too late. Nourry was in the gutter. His blood was flowing—his carotid artery had been sliced by a knife!"

An exclamation of horror emerged from every mouth.

"Is he dead?" asked the President breathlessly.

"In our arms, without having said a word."

"And the drunkards?" asked the calm voice of Rouletabille.

"They ran away. Our agents are searching the vicinity—the entire quarter—but I'll tell you something terrible, Monsieur le Président... it won't astonish me if I don't catch them. I believe that it was planned."

"You don't need to believe it, Monsieur le Directeur, you can be sure of it!" Rouletabille declared, turning to his boss to add: "Didn't I tell you that three of us won't be too many, against *them*?"

Chapter XVIII
Tango

The day after that memorable meeting, at about eight o'clock in the evening, a certain *poilu* of our acquaintance could be seen wandering, pipe in mouth, through all the streets adjacent to the major boulevards, from the Rue de Helder to the Rue Royale. He went into almost all the bars—or, at least, those frequented by so-called elegant clientele of foreigners that the war had not chased out of Paris, or who had returned to it "since the Marne."

If the *poilu* in question had ordered "a glass" in each of those establishments he would have needed an exceptional constitution to be able to continue on his way with such an assured stride as the one that finally brought him a small tavern in the Rue Caumartin, in front of a counter on which he leaned his elbows in a melancholy fashion.

For the tenth time in two hours he asked for "a quarter of Vittel," for Rouletabille (it was him) was naturally sober, especially when he was working—and we catch him here in mid-endeavor.

He addressed himself to an amiable, slightly plump lady who must have been pretty twenty years earlier, and who was meticulously supervising the distribution of cocktails and other drinks to a mixed clientele of which the weaker sex was not, all things considered, the finest ornament.

Those ladies, like the "patronne," were generally of a certain age, while the young people were decidedly young; Rouletabille thought that he recognized some of them by virtue of having seen them, in the months before the war, gliding over the floors of "tea-dances" with a grace that ought to have brought them twenty francs at the end of the day.

"Pardon me, Madame, could you tell me whether Vladimir Féodorovitch will be here this evening?"

"Professor Vladimir?" the plump lady replied, patting the curls of her red wig. "There's every chance Monsieur le Poilu! Look—just yesterday at this time, he was dining at that table."

"Do you think he'll come back to dine this evening?"

"Oh, it's quite probable—unless he's been invited to dine in town by his princess."

"Oh yes—Princess Botosani."

"Oh, you know about her..."

"I know that he's a fellow who keep beautiful company—isn't he, Madame?"

"You don't say! Professor Vladimir isn't just anyone, and he doesn't give his lessons to just anyone. They're mad about him in high society. Oh, the war has done him a great deal of harm, but he's no fool, and he gets by all the same. He has to."

"Madame, I have a magnificent proposition to put to Vladimir Féodorovitch, and I'd be very grateful to you if you could give me his address."

"His address? Why, Monsieur, it's here, and in all the chic bars of the neighborhood. This is where he has his correspondence sent."

Rouletabille cast his eyes over the letters that she showed him. Their postmarks indicated that they had been there for several days. Becoming impatient, he asked point-blank: "Where is Vladimir dancing to-night?"

"Eh! You know full well, my lad, that the tango-bars have been closed since the war started."

"I know that—but I'm also not unaware that there are some that open clandestinely. Speak! You can do so with confidence, and I assure you that it's in Vladimir's interest—an important affair. Where is he dancing?"

"Where he's dancing they won't let you in dressed as a *poilu*."

"Don't worry about that—tell me, quickly."

"Well, you'll find Vladimir, from ten o'clock onwards, in a small place on the Rue de Balzac, whose exact number I don't recall, but which you'll easily recognize by the quantity of automobiles bringing the enthusiasts. It's where the painter Chéron[20] used to live. Do you know it?"

"I know it," Rouletabille replied, getting to his feet. Thank you, and au revoir."

An hour later, he was outside the house in question. He had put on his most elegant civilian clothes, but had not abandoned his pipe.

It was a dark night, in a dark street. The house itself only emerged from the opaque shadows when the headlights of an automobile illuminated it. The auto stopped, a couple got out; a little door on the left-hand side of the house opened; the couple disappeared and the auto drew away, going to park a hundred meters further on.

Arrivals were becoming increasingly numerous.

---

[20] Presumably Louis Chéron (1660-1725), although he left France in 1685 when the Edict of Nantes was revoked (he was a Protestant) and became a naturalized British citizen.

As he slipped along the sidewalk, the reporter heard muffled music: the languorous and long-drawn-out echo of the tangos of yesteryear.

They're crazy, the reporter thought, *but then, the must be gambling as well as dancing in there.*

Rouletabille reflected that it was impossible that the police were unaware of these little nocturnal gatherings, but that it was in their interests to let them enjoy a semblance of security for a while in order to capture certain interesting individuals who were likely to hang about in such a shady milieu.

He had taken care to note the fashion in which the new arrivals knocked on the little door: three raps, then one then two. No one rang. He knocked in his turn.

The door opened. An old woman, doubtless the concierge, asked him what he wanted. He replied that he had come to see Vladimir Féodorovitch, and even affirmed that he had arranged a rendezvous with him.

The concierge showed him into a small room summarily furnished with a table and two chairs.

Rouletabille did not have to wait long. Vladimir arrived almost immediately and, on seeing him, as had been his custom in days of old when he wanted to express his joy, set about prancing like a ballerina, sketching with his long legs what vulgar choreography calls a "pigeon wing."

"Rouletabille! That's nice! You're no longer in the trenches, then?"

"What about you?"

Vladimir stopped dancing. He looked at Rouletabille obliquely while shaking his hand. He was not entirely sure whether the other was joking. Smiling in his silly fashion, he replied: "Oh, me, I'm an 'undesirable.'"

"You haven't been called up in Russia?"

"Did you really believe, my dear chap, that I'm Russian? Well, I too believed that I was Russian—but can you imagine that, at the outbreak of hostilities, when I was ready to do my duty like everyone else, a funny thing happened to me, about which I'll tell you..."

"If it stopped you becoming a soldier, you must have suffered a great deal, Vladimir."

"Don't be so sarcastic, Rouletabille—I've always liked war, myself, and I have no fear of adventures, as you know very well. All the same, I'd be in agreement with you regarding the military question and I don't mind admitting to you that it wouldn't entirely have pleased me to make war as a soldier, having only previously done so as a reporter—which requires less discipline."

"It's true, Vladimir, that you've never been very disciplined."

"Is it? I didn't tell you that. But when one's a soldier and one isn't very disciplined, the profession, according to what I've been told, isn't without a certain redoubtable inconvenience..."

"Bah! One only appears before a firing-squad once!" Rouletabille observed, vaguely, amused by Vladimir's increasing embarrassment and the entanglement of his explanations."

"Very kind of you! I don't like the idea of being shot at all, so I won't hide it from you that when I suddenly noticed, on looking at my identity papers more closely and making a serious study of them, that my personal status..."

"Your personal status! You're well-read in international law, Vladimir!"

"My God—it's certainly been necessary for me to study it with a few obliging jurisconsultants… and it was then that I learned that, because of a certain incomplete naturalization of one of my ancestors, that I've never been Russian…"

"Really? What are you, then, Vladimir?"

"I'm quite simply Rumanian."

"Quite simply!" Rouletabille repeated, unable to help smiling. "Be careful! Examine your papers well, Vladimir—there's a rumor going around about Rumania's entry into the war…"

Vladimir shook his head. "No, no! I have information about that. Rumania will remain neutral, I tell you."

"And who told you?"

"A certain Wallachian princess who's very well in with Enver Pacha."

"Really? So you're still hanging around with princesses, Vladimir? And on that subject, might I ask for news of yours? How is Madame Vladimir?"

"She's dead."

"As you foresaw, as I recall, and also as her advanced age and taste for strong liquor might have caused one to dread, if my memory serves me right."

"What I did not foresee, my dear chap, is that the woman I believed to be as rich as the Queen of Sheba would die without leaving me a sou, the slut!"

"Bah! You're still young. Marry Princess Botosani…"

"Oh, you've heard about that!" said Vladimir, swelling with pride. "By the way, I haven't asked you for news of Madame Rouletabille. Still with Radko Dimitrieff?"

Rouletabille did not reply. The whole world knew that the illustrious Bulgarian Ivana Vichlikoff, who had married the *L'Époque* reporter after resounding adventures, had abandoned the cause of the felon king long before Ferdinand's treason, and had followed the patriotic general who had put his sword at the service of the Tsar to Russia, in the life-or-death struggle of the Slavic races. In that tempest, Rouletabille's love for his young wife had been obliged to suffer the fatality that separates a lovingly united household.

"Let's go downstairs," said Rouletabille. "There's not much excitement here."

They went down.

In a vast room that opened on to the back of the house, which had been the painter' studio, a certain quantity of small tables had been disposed at which the obligatory champagne was being served (at thirty francs a bottle.) The crowd was however, joyful, and devoid of scandal. It was recognized among men and women of the world that people danced. The tango, moreover, renders gravity; and the most flirtatious of young women, as soon as they begin to dance it, resume the inspired but concentrated expression that characterizes the adepts of the new choreography.

That entirely exceptional "underworld" of wartime Paris was, as one might well imagine, far from seductive to Rouletabille even though he was no prude.

The two young men sat down at a table near the orchestra, which comprised a pianist and three violinists. The latter were not wearing red jackets or speaking Hungarian. It was necessary to drink champagne, which did not displease Vladimir at all. To begin with, they talked about "this and that."

"It's a long time since you've seen La Candeur?" asked the Slav.

"I haven't had an opportunity to see him since the war broke out," Rouletabille replied.

"And he hasn't written to you?"

"I certainly haven't received anything."

"I'll tell you the reason for his silence in your regard, Rouletabille—La Candeur is quite simply ashamed! La Candeur has got himself a cushy job behind the lines, in the automobile service. La Candeur is nothing more or less than a shirker."

"That's disgusting," said Rouletabille, without frowning.

"Absolutely disgusting," agreed Vladimir, with a magnificent unconsciousness of his own situation. "I haven't had the opportunity to tell him what I think, but if I run into him..."

"You'd be quite right," said Rouletabille, "and it won't be undeserved."

Then they fell silent, vaguely watching the dancers. Rouletabille was astonished that the Slav was not dancing, and told him so,

"My dear chap," Vladimir whispered in his ear, "I've promised my princess not to dance with anyone but her—and she hasn't arrived yet! All these ladies are annoyed with me, but I can surely make a sacrifice for that charming woman—who, in any case, is leaving Paris in a week."

"Oh yes? Where is she going?"

"To Rumania! But just between us, she's going to Turkey."

"She's consented to a separation from you?"

"Oh, she'll come back as soon as possible…and it's necessary that you know that the end of the war is much closer than is generally believed."

"Did she tell you that?"

"She did—and, still between the two of us, I can tell you"—Vladimir leaned toward Rouletabille's ear—"what Enver Pacha told her. Enver Pacha told her himself that the Boche have found an invention so extraordinary that, within a matter of months, nothing—nothing, you hear—will be able to resist them!"

"Bah! And this invention is serious?"

"She was very serious when she told me, my dear chap!"

After that, there was a rather long pause.

"What are you thinking about?" Vladimir asked, eventually.

"I'm thinking about you, Vladimir, and the misapprehension you're under relative to Rumania's plans. It will enter the war before long; I can assure you of that—and from the moment that I tell you, you know that it can be taken for granted."

"Damn!" said Vladimir. "That's serious!"

"The matter is too serious, where you're concerned," Rouletabille replied, "for me to joke about it. Just think that, if you don't go back to Rumania then, you'll be considered in France to be a deserter and treated as such. Isn't that frightful?"

"Which is to say that you're frightening me. Personally, I don't see why, having not taken up arms for France or for Russia, I should get myself killed for Rumania!"

"The reasoning seems sound to me," Rouletabille agreed. "Hold on, though, Vladimir—I'm sure that when you go home, if you examine your identity papers…"

"Of course! That's what I'm going to do tomorrow. And I'll find my jurisconsultant again. You can't imagine how complicated my persona status is!"

"I'm sure," Rouletabille continued, "that you might well discover that you're quite simply Turkish—all the more so as you speak Turkish as if it were your mother tongue."

"Why Turkish? Turkey's in the war! That would cause many difficulties."

"There are no difficulties in that direction, when one has money," Rouletabille replied, "for you know full well that, with money, one doesn't become a soldier in Turkey."

"Yes," said Vladimir, "But I don't have any money."

"If that's all it is, I can lend you some," said the reporter.

"You like me a little, don't you, Rouletabille?" said the Slav, hesitantly. "And... and...you're rich, then?"

"I have, in truth, a great deal of affection for you, Vladimir, and I prove it by continuing to associate with you in spite of your faults, which are enormous. As regards the money question, I can tell you that I'm more at my ease, and that you shall have all the money you need."

"What for?" asked Vladimir, increasingly astonished.

"To get by in Turkey, of course! Didn't you tell me that you're going to become Turkish and go to Turkey with your Princess Botosani, who knows Enver Pacha so well?"

"Oh—yes, I did tell you that..."

The Slav fixed the reporter with eyes shining with intelligence. Suddenly, Rouletabille got to his feet, put his hand on Vladimir's shoulder and said: "Let's go smoke a cigarette in the garden."

There was a large garden behind the house; the light of the moon, which had just risen, showed it to be utterly deserted. The two young men plunged into the hornbeams.

"A Turk and a friend of Enver Pacha!" said Rouletabille, emphatically. "That's lucky, my friend! Enver is a gallant man who can refuse nothing to women, and since Princess Botosani is so intelligent and so…intriguing, it won't take long for you to be given some confidential mission—from which, in that country, one invariably comes back padded with gold!"

"I'd like to be padded with gold!" sighed Vladimir. "Tell me what I have to do, Rouletabille, to be padded with gold!"

"Very little, my friend, I assure you. For example: travel the world in luxury trains, allowing oneself to be coddled, pampered and entertained. For in truth, is there any existence more agreeable than that of a gentleman who arrives in a foreign land, charged by his government to negotiate an arms deal, and having the power to increase its magnitude? One does everything to make that man content! One ties oneself in knots as soon as he formulates any desire! And as one is absolutely determined that he will retain an excellent memory of his journey, one does not let him leave without at least giving him what is necessary to put together an entire gold-lined wardrobe if, like you, he has dreamed of one day returning to his beloved fatherland padded with that precious metal."

"Be quiet, if you're not talking seriously, Rouletabille, for you're opening horizons to me—horizons! I can already see myself at Krupp's, as the representative of young Turkey! With Princess Botosani, Rouletabille, anything is possible."

"And with you, Vladimir, is everything possible?"

The Slav did not answer immediately. Then, abruptly, he said: "No, not that! No, I can't! To serve the Turks is to serve the Boche, Rouletabille—and that I'll never do! Perhaps what I'm going to tell you isn't very marvelous. Can you imagine that in the early days of September 1914, when the first Uhlan patrols weren't far from the Eiffel Tower...oh, can you imagine that I wept? Yes, I wept at the thought that the Boche were going to doom Paris! I love your Paris more than you can imagine, you who only know me under a rather 'devil-may-care' appearance, and that only certain foreigners can comprehend who have come here once and gone far away, but who always think: I love simply Paris for the pleasure of seeing it, which it gave me! I love Paris because it's the most chic place in the world...and I'll never do anything to harm Paris. That's the way it is!"

Vladimir fell silent. Rouletabille shook his hand in the darkness. "Indeed it is. But what if you were to do something *for* Paris?"

"Of course—and with what joy, what enthusiasm! Especially...especially, Rouletabille, if I were to be working with you!"

The reporter drew Vladimir deeper into the hornbeams.

Twenty minutes later, when they came back to the threshold of the light poured out by the rooms where people were dancing, Vladimir's face was particularly grave. The two young men exchanged another firm handshake. Then Vladimir suddenly said: "She's here!" and went swiftly into the drawing-room.

Rouletabille went back into the ballroom as well, to see the Slav sketching the first moves of a two-step, in company with a heavily made-up and somewhat exotically beautiful young woman.

Rouletabille asked a bystander: "That's Princess Botosani, isn't it?"

"Yes, she's infatuated with Vladimir Féodorovitch. These great ladies, honestly—nothing gets in their way!"

The reporter stayed there for a few moments, studying the princess with great attention, then paid his bill and left the house.

He went back on foot to his small apartment overlooking the Jardins du Luxembourg.

He worked all night, went to bed at five a.m., and was woken up at nine by Vladimir. The two young men remained locked away until noon. At twelve, they reemerged.

Rouletabille went out in his military uniform, leapt into a cab, and had himself taken to a restaurant in the vicinity of the Avenue de Clichy that was renowned for its tripe, prepared in the Caen style.

Chapter IX
Behind the Lines

Outside the door, a superb general-staff limousine was parked. Rouletabille cast an eye over the magnificent automobile, observing that the chauffeur was neither in his seat nor on the sidewalk, and went into the establishment. He went past the famous steaming boilers, climbed a staircase, went into a large hall, and immediately perceived, sitting at a small table by a window overlooking the Avenue de Clichy, a military man of imposing stature and corpulence, dressed in immaculate horizon-blues, whose sleeve was ornamented by an armband bearing a large capital A.

That enormous warrior was so busy having the contents of the dishes placed nearby on a warming-plate on to his own plate that he did not even look up when the newcomer came to take possession of the vacant chair at his table. It was not until that unexpected guest sat down directly opposite his plate that he deigned to take notice of the unusual presence.

"Rouletabille!" he exclaimed—and immediately got up, so abruptly that he nearly tipped everything over. He seized the reporter in his arms and hugged him to his mighty bosom.

"Take care, La Candeur!" said Rouletabille. "You're stifling me!"

"Oh, let me embrace you! It's been such a long time" My God, you look well! I fear that the trenches...but let's sit down...let's not let the tripe get cold! You'll eat with me? But what miracle brings you here?"

Freed from the benevolent giant's grip, Rouletabille replied that he was as hungry as a wolf, and that they could chat over dessert.

"Eat, old chap, eat! I'm on my third portion, you know, and my third bottle of cider. Oh, Rouletabille, you don't know what an appetite the work I'm doing gives me!"

"Yes, yes, I know that one's very busy in the general staff's automobiles."

"Oh, you have no idea! One's on the go all the time, my dear boy! And it's necessary to be very sober, you know! And always running errands—for in this job, one has to do everything, even doing the colonel's shopping in the big stores. You have no idea, I tell you!"

And the giant sighed, causing the rest of his plateful to disappear—and ordering two more.

"I can see that you're very unhappy, deep down, my poor La Candeur. And in truth, I grieve for you. But isn't it your own fault, to some extent? Why didn't you come with us to the trenches? One has leisure time in the trenches! Not to mention that one isn't poorly nourished, by any means! And one has time to play cards—your passion!"

"Yes, I'm told that there are some good games there." Visibly embarrassed by the direction in which Rouletabille was taking the conversation, La Candeur went on: "Speaking of cards, do you have any news of that animal Vladimir?"

"None! It's ages since I've seen him; I've had no more news of him than of you! And you pretend that you love me!"

La Candeur's face went crimson. He raised an enormous fist above the table. "Me! I don't love you?"

Rouletabille stopped the fist, which would have smashed everything. "Calm down, La Candeur, and answer me."

"I'll answer you right away," said La Candeur, who was stammering and seemed to be about to choke. "When war was declared, things happened so fast that we didn't even have time to see one another. We were separated immediately...me, I was in the transport service...I swear to you, Rouletabille, that I did everything I could to join you! Finally, I resigned myself to it. It was only when I had been convinced that it was impossible for me, by any means, to go and fight by your side, having had a few difficulties with my superiors because of two horses that had been killed under me..."

"What!" Rouletabille exclaimed. "You've had two horses killed beneath you, and you don't have the *croix de guerre*?"

"My God, they were very small horses, which had no resistance...you understand? I only had to sit on them, and that was that!"

"Yes, yes, they were flattened and died."

"Something like that. Anyway, they didn't have any reason to give me the *croix de guerre*. That was when I had the idea that, since I couldn't ride a horse without some misfortune overtaking it, it would be preferable all round if I manned an automobile! I had a few connections...I used them...and that's the whole story. Now, I'll tell you, just between the two of us, that I'm not a mighty warrior...far from it...and you know that full well, and I couldn't go with you...so I'll admit to you that I'm not too upset that things worked out the way they did, since I couldn't go with you..."

Rouletabille looked La Candeur in the face. The latter's disturbance only increased. And suddenly, the *Époque* reporter decided to speak.

"La Candeur, I've come to tell you that your troubles are over—you can come with me now!"

The giant took the blow bravely. He did not faint, although, all in all, he loved Rouletabille so much that might have been overcome with joy. He could not speak for some time, though and he began going red and pale by turns, an obvious sign of great emotion.

Finally, he was able to say: "You're not joking?"

"Do I look as if I'm joking?"

In fact, Rouletabille had never seemed so serous. He was now looking at La Candeur as seriously as possible.

"It's not necessary," Rouletabille said, "for that to stop you eating."

"No thanks—I've finished. You've…cut off my appetite. I'll wait a little. I'm so surprised…and glad…"

"You're sure that you're glad?"

"I'd put my hand in the fire! Obviously, I'm all of a dither…but that must be gladness. I love you so much, Rouletabille…"

The latter did not smile. He knew perfectly well what was going through the worthy giant's mind. He did not doubt the immense amity that the giant had for him, but he also knew that his incredible timidity had made La Candeur an individual who was not very combative, in spite of his redoubtable appearance. Certainly, at critical moments, La Candeur was brave, and had often proved it—but outside of those critical moments, he did not believe in his own bravery! So, the battle that was going on in the heart of his vast friend, whose ups and downs Rouletabille could follow very well, made him feel genuinely tender. He knew that friendship would emerge victorious from the struggle; he would appreciate La Candeur's devotion all the more in consequence.

The end of the meal was calm—all the calmer because La Candeur was no longer eating or drinking. From time to time, in a grave tone, he asked for details of the life led by the troopers in the trenches, the dangers they ran, the intensity of the bombardment, and the science of the cooks.

Rouletabille answered him calmly and untiringly. When the time came to get up from the table, however, he said to his friend: "Are you so very interested, then, in the life one leads in the trenches, La Candeur?"

"What? Of course it interests me—isn't it understood that from now on. I'll be leading that life with you?"

"With me? But I'm not going back to the trenches!"

"Where are you going, then?"

"My dear La Candeur, we're both going to a sewing-machine factory!"

"A sewing-machine factory?"

They had arrived on the sidewalk beside the magnificent general-staff automobile. Planted in front of Rouletabille, La Candeur stood there open-mouthed, utterly bewildered.

"Well, what, La Candeur? Don't you want to go to a sewing-machine factory?"

"Yes, yes…damn it! But obviously, I'm wondering why?"

Rouletabille leaned closer to the giant's ear. "It seems that the State has, at present, a great need for sewing-machines."

"Really?"

"Just as I say."

"But I've never manufactured sewing-machines myself."

"Well, you'll learn."

La Candeur let out an enormous laugh, and clapped Rouletabille on the shoulder so hard that the latter had to hold on to the automobile in order not to end up in the gutter.

"Sewing-machines! Sewing-machines! We're in sewing-machines now? Oh, how novel, old man! Well, it'll need a long trip in the Bois to get me over so much excitement. Let's go take our constitutional, Rouletabille!" And he invited the reporter to take the seat next to him. He drew off at speed immediately, repeating like a joyful litany: Sewing-machines! Sewing-machines!"

At the corner of the Avenue du Bois they nearly crashed into a beautiful car whose chauffeur was copiously cursed by La Candeur—but all of a sudden, the latter exclaimed; "Rouletabille! Look into that car!"

Rouletabille had already seen and recognized Princess Botosani and, by her side, relaxing on the cushions, the handsome Vladimir...

La Candeur sat up in his seat and shouted at his former companion in adventure: "It's all right for some, behind the lines!"

Chapter X
Essen

Essen! Essen! Rouletabille finally caught sight of Essen.

For more than an hour, already, the train that was carrying him had been going through a landscape that he knew well, but which he no longer recognized. He recalled his previous astonishment at the prodigious activity of that human inferno. What could be said about it today?

Where there had once been a city, he found a world. The *feldwebel*, behind him, who was watching him and permitted him to put his nose out of the window, gave him he details.

Before the war, Essen had had less than 30,000 inhabitants. Now it had more than a million, and 120,000 of those citizens worked in the factories night and day. The latter now employed at least 300,000 workers, 60,000 of whom were women, working n shifts night and day.

The *feldwebel* told him all that with pride, and certainly under orders, undoubtedly to lower the morale of the prisoners he was guarding...but Rouletabille's morale was solid.

The reporter had not lost any time since the day when, in Paris, he had been given the word to "go!" He had overcome difficulties of every sort.

To begin with, Nourry's murder had been a veritable disaster for Rouletabille. Nourry would have been able to furnish him with a hundred precious details regarding the life of the prisoners at Essen and the conditions of their work in the factories. Rouletabille would have been able to extract from his still-recent memories all kinds of things useful to his enterprise; he might have found a departure-point therein for one of those flights of the imagination with which the reporter was accustomed to confront material obstacles that would have been insurmountable for anyone else.

Nourry no longer being there to supply him with information, Rouletabille had been obliged to consult various people, including engineers, who, having only visited Krupp's before the war, and who had only seen there what people wanted them to see.

A few conversations that he had had in private with Madame Fulbert had not told him anything new about the *Titania* itself, but he knew—and it was particularly important to him—that Nicole Fulbert had worked closely with her father, and that she was not unacquainted with the whole of the inventor's secret.

Finally, before going into a sewing-machine factory with La Candeur, Rouletabille has assumed another face, another identity. He had allowed his beard to grow and now wore spectacles. That summary transformation of his physiognomy rendered him quite unrecognizable, making him into a different man.

That other man was named Michel Talmar, and was in possession of identity papers attesting that for five years he had been the supervisor of a workshop at Blin and Company, one of the foremost sewing-machine factories in France.

Rouletabille had worked in that establishment night and day for three weeks. We shall soon see why he had chosen it—and, in truth, he had not been wasting his time.

Naturally, La Candeur had gone with him to Blin's. The gentle giant had devoted himself to the manufacture of particular components, rather delicate in nature, many of which he had broken like wisps of straw to begin with, before succeeding in mastering the work. He did not understand his sudden change of situation, but he was with Rouletabille, and that consideration took precedence over all others. His amazement, bewilderment and despair are easily imaginable when the moment came for Rouletabille to explain to him that he had only been introduced to a sewing-machine factory in order to send him to Essen, and when he discovered the route that he would have to take to arrive more surely at Krupp's—initially, via the trenches...

Afterwards...oh, afterwards! Firstly, in a little skirmish ahead of the lines, arranged expressly for him, he had to be skillful enough to get himself taken prisoner by the Boche! It was forbidden for him to be killed or wounded!

"If you follow the plan exactly," Rouletabille had told him, by way of consolation, "our separation, which you're lamenting, will only be brief. Don't forget to tell the first *feldwebel* with whom you have dealings that you've been working with sewing-machines all your life. It appears that it's the surest means of being sent to Essen, where we'll meet up again!"

"Why not send us there together? Why separate us?" La Candeur had groaned, stubbornly.

"In order not to awaken any suspicion! I'll get myself captured at another part of the front. Don't worry about me!"

"And what are we going to do in Essen? Can you tell me?"

"But I've already told you, my dear La Candeur—we're going to make sewing-machines."

"Yes, yes—understood. Yet another coup, after your fashion."

The operation, well-planned and directed by Rouletabille, had been a complete success. La Candeur had been taken prisoner without sustaining overmuch damage to his person.

It had not been the same for Rouletabille. The reporter had contrived to be captured at Verdun, in a tunnel that he had chosen himself as the most appropriate for his endeavor. The men in the trench had named the tunnel "the international" because part of it belonged to the French and part to the Germans. Toward the middle, a few bags of earth had been thrown down, behind which the sentinels kept watch, a few paces away from one another. The Boche sentinel and the French sentinel sometimes chatted with one another. Rouletabille now spoke German fluently, having learned it since his marriage, Ivana being something of a polyglot.

The reporter had agreed with the Boche soldier that there as a very simple and interesting means for both of them to put an end to the dangers of the war; they had only to have themselves taken prisoner, him by the Boche and the other by the French. Passing over the bags, they would crossed over en route and advance, shouting: "Kamerad!"

The Boche sentinel had agreed enthusiastically, and Rouletabille had begun to carry out the plan agreed by the two parties—but he had no sooner gone past the sentinel than he latter, turning round, had hurled a grenade at him.

The reporter had been knocked down and wounded in the shoulder. Taken prisoner, he had immediately been evacuated to Rastatt and had remained there for a fortnight.

The wound was not serious, but what was more serious was the lost time. When it had healed, or nearly so, his anxiety only increased, because, in spite of the information he had been given, the famous sewing-machine trick did not seem, after all, to be succeeding. At any rate, he did not receive any offer of work.

Another week had gone by in that fashion, and the reporter had begun to work on an entirely different plan, which consisted of escaping from Rastatt and getting to Essen by means of nocturnal marches...but what a difference there would then be between what he still had to do and what he might have hoped to achieve had the Boche introduced himself into the place themselves!

Then, suddenly, one evening when, in desperation, he was about to put his escape plan into operation, the sewing-machine plan had come together! Someone came to ask him whether he would like to work in his trade, and offered him a salary of three marks a day. He accepted, and as put on a train for Essen. Nourry's information was sound—and Rouletabille's plan had been excellent!

Now the reporter said to himself: *As long as La Candeur has had as much success as me and I find him out there! With the worthy giant, God's help and that of the amiable hooligan Vladimir, we can get to work in earnest!*

Essen! Essen! A gigantic vision! A fantastic, infernal vision! The train carrying Rouletabille was now penetrating into the very heart of that inferno. What he had gone through until now had only been preparation for this nightmare. Hundreds of enormous chimneys spitting incalculable amounts of smoke into the sky, which veiled the face of the sun, stopping its says, and pouring a rain of ash and scoria down upon the city, as a volcanic eruption does—except that, whereas volcanoes sometimes pause, Essen never stops. The god Krupp is more powerful than Vulcan, and the masters of the mythological forge were small beer compared with our modern arms-manufacturers.

From the moment when the train pulled into the station, the noise of the city became even more deafening; the whistling of the locomotives and the tocsin of trams was abruptly joined by the howling of sirens, and then the distant sound of artillery-fire coming from the range. The bass-line to that prodigious racket was the powerful and continuous sound emitted by the factories: the monstrous respiration of the Hydra with five hundred mouths of flame!

Rouletabille was stunned by it. He had expected something formidable, but what he saw and heard surpassed all imagination. The twenty French prisoners who had made the journey with him allowed themselves, in their bewilderment, to be shoved, jostled and insulted by their guards.

Rouletabille had expected that they would first be taken to the camp that Nourry had mentioned, but he soon perceived that he was being taken in a westerly direction, toward the factories. He and his companions were advancing between the soldiers, who had bayonets fitted to their rifles, under the direction of a territorial *feldwebel* about whom the prisoners had had few complaints to make during the journey.

Although it was Sunday, and very early in the morning, the streets were full of workers who were all heading in the same westerly direction. They were obviously going to relieve the night shift crews. Men were coming from all directions, as if springing from the ground.

The entire black swarm marched without an exclamation, without even whispering. Innumerable footfalls could be heard on the paving stones. The little troop in which the reporter was place was drawn along by the mute turbulence.

That somber army going silently to its frightful work, between the black and smoky facades of houses, before which the lamentable squares of little ragged gardens were displayed like items of dirty laundry, made a sinister impression.

As they came closer to the factories, the gaze was interrupted by enormous cast-iron conduits that crossed the streets from one wall to the other, connecting the workshops and blocking the horizon at second-floor level. Finally, they came to a wall, and to one of the hundred gates guarded by firemen in red caps on sentry duty, who watched over the workers with the most active vigilance.

The little troop stopped at the porter's lodge. The flowing river of workers was engulfed beneath the portico.

Rouletabille had placed himself in such a way as not to miss any of what was happening during the entry of the workers. Each of them, on going in, unhooked a piece of metal bearing a number from an immense blackboard. Doubtless the worker had to hand it to the foreman on arrival at the workshop; then, it would be handed back at the end of the shift and replaced here, in a container that was shaped like an enormous letterbox—and into which, indeed, a crew emerging hastily at that moment, was throwing its numbers. The next day, each one would find the number in the same place as the day before, and no one would escape being counted.

Finally, the *feldwebel* made a sign, and the prisoners started marching again. At that moment, Rouletabille's emotion was at its peak. He was about to penetrate into the jealously-guarded world of the factories, and it was the Boche themselves who were about to introduce him to it.

So perfect a realization of his plan filled him with such joy that he had to make an effort to hide it. He had feared so much that he might be forced to work by night, or in the dark, hiding himself, at the risk of a thousand perils, in the region of fog, soot and iron that stretched from Dusseldorf to Dortmund, passing through Elberfeld, Duisburg, Mulheim, Solingem and Oberhausen, of which Essen was merely a district, and of which the factories of Essen were the mighty heart!

Now, the enemy had taken the trouble to deposit him, Rouletabille, in the very shadow of the *Titania*.

They went through the gate. They were in the lair of the beast!

They were immediately taken into a small room where they had to undergo a minute inspection; it was the fifth of that kind since Rouletabille had been in the custody of the Boche, but this time, the liberties taken and demands made by the redoubtable inquisition were unable to irritate the young man.

The first things that he read on the walls of Krupp were repeated on multiple posters: *Hüttet euch vor espionen und espioninnen...*

Understood, the reporter said to himself. *We'll watch out for spies of both sexes! Go on, look! Nothing in the hands, nothing in the pockets...*

Now they were going through the factory.

First there was an immense courtyard furrowed by rails, cluttered with engines and debris, covered with steel bars and machine-parts.

Then there was a stroll through an increasingly deafening racket along the interminable walls. Then there were more yards to cross, steel conduits to step over, tracks to avoid, monstrous machines to go round, while the fire of hell were roaring in giant chimneys and, from time to time, visions of demons in floods of flame surging forth as the door of a workshop opened.

Finally, at the very center, or at least in the core, of the Krupp establishments, the little troop came to a halt in front of a huge barracks of smoke-blackened brick. They were taken into a crumbling vestibule, whose cracked walls were held up by new beams. The *feldwebel* took went on to a sordid stairway and called out to someone; another NCO appeared on the greasy black steps. They exchanged pieces of paper and proceeded to take a roll-call of the prisoners.

Michel Talmar was the first to answer: "Present!" He was immediately escorted by an aged soldier to a lugubrious dormitory. There as a long succession of rooms there, which, the chatty old territorial explained, had once served as a dormitory for unmarried workmen; more recently, the rooms had been devoted to the lodging of prisoners of war who worked in the factory.

So Rouletabille was to sleep in the factory itself! Oh, how richly rewarded he had been for the flash of genius that had suddenly shown him the use he could make of the passage in Nourry's story in which the latter had mentioned the manufacture of sewing-machines at Essen! If only he could set eyes on La Candeur! He darted glances into al he rooms whose doors stood ajar, but they were empty. At this hour, the prisoners were in the workshops.

It was to the far end of the corridor, to the last door on the right, that Rouletabille was taken. His territorial gave him a sign to indicate that he had arrived. He had, however, to wait in the corridor for his companions in captivity before going into the room.

The latter arrived and halted in their turn before the doors that were indicated to them by the *feldwebel*. The corridor was only guarded at the two ends. In response to an order, everyone disappeared into the rooms. There was a window in each room. The daylight that penetrated by that route was poor. Rouletabille observed, in fact, that the courtyard at the center of which his barracks were built was surrounded by tall black buildings. It was not through there that he would catch a glimpse of the monstrous edifice in whose flanks the Boche were hiding the *Titania*.

Since he had been in Essen he had thought about nothing else, but in vain; at every street corner, in every square, and over walls his gaze had sought a part of that gigantic building, but nothing had reminded him of the fantastic monument of which Nourry had spoken.

He turned round and studied the little corner in which he was to live and rest between hours of work attentively. There were ten green-painted iron beds there, low and covered in a grey cloth. Beds! Those who consented to work at Krupp's were definitely cared for, and spoiled!

Against the walls were seven narrow cupboards, portraits of the emperor and the empress, and those of the Krupps—the father white-bearded with a slender nose, energetic eyes, firm and angular features; the son, the most recent, fat, with an indecisive expression, devoid of will-power, sad and mild, with spectacles perched on his nose. Between the portraits were placards bearing the eternal inscription: *Hüttet euch vor espionen und espioninnen...*

That advice, once addressed to German workers and now addressed to French prisoners, made the young man smile again.

The beds were almost touching. That was the only furniture. It was reproduced exactly in all the rooms, as Rouletabille was able to observe through the windows in the doors. All the doors had windows in, thus facilitating surveillance.

The *feldwebel* who was responsible for the floor, like a floor-manager in a fashionable hotel, was a fat man about fifty years of age, with a brick-red face barred by an enormous white moustache, which bobbed up and down untiringly as he rolled his terrible eyes. He was not a bad man to impose on prisoners, and was presumably a good father, as Rouletabille judged to begin with, when he saw him enter the room and heard him call out in re-sounding and comminatory terms the principal points of the interior regulations.

Rouletabille received the number 284. He was to occupy bed 9. They got up at five and went to bed at nine. From nine on absolute silence was obligatory. Nat-urally, each prisoner made his own bed and washed his own linen. He received eighty pfennigs per day, lodg-ings, a blanket, and a pair of sheets every three weeks. They were spoiled! Spoiled!

A whistle-blast resounded in the corridor. It ap-peared that soup was being served for the new arrivals. Behind the *feldwebel*, the young men went into a large room; there was one of that kind for every five dormitories or rooms like the one to which Rouletabille had been assigned.

There too were the inevitable four portraits, the notice regarding spies, and a long table surrounded by stools. A rather rudimentary breakfast was served to the travelers, who had not eaten since noon the previous day, and who were dying of hunger. A table and chairs! They were definitely being treated as workers rather than prisoners! The table was set! A deep plate of enameled iron, a fork and a wrought iron spoon! What luxury!

The soup, served by old women who arrived from the kitchens, was some kind of stew, in which a few morsels of unidentifiable meat were floating, and five hundred grams of bread for the day, water at their discretion—but they had the option of having beer sent up from the canteen. At the end of the meal there was a little water tasting of acorns, which pretended to be coffee. But what did that matter to Rouletabille? He was hardly preoccupied with nourishment.

The brick-tinted *feldwebel*, who was glad to hear a Frenchman speaking German, prided himself on being able to understand and speak a little French. He said Rouletabille, who, while thinking about something else entirely, seemed to be looking at his plate unenthusiastically: "*Ja. Ja*—sad! That's war for you!"

After breakfast, they were shown, still on the same floor, a room with a few greasy bathtubs, and another with a central trough in which the prisoners could wash their own linen Rouletabille took advantage of finding himself standing beside the *feldwebel* to ask: "We do everything here? We never go out?"

"Never—unless it's to go to the workshops or walk in the courtyard—but no one ever goes out of the factory—*nie und nimmermehr*!"

"Well, that's me informed."

They were allowed to freshen up. They were allowed to go into the common rooms—the bathroom, the laundry and the dining-room—but could not go anywhere else, except their rooms, without risking court-martial. On the *feldwebel*'s orders, Rouletabille had to explain that part of the regulations to his companions in captivity.

After the ablutions, therefore, the reporter went back to his room—or, rather, his dormitory—not to sleep, but to think.

Chapter XI
Rouletabille Gets His Bearings

Two months had gone by since Nourry had told his story. At that time, Fulbert had considered that, within five months, the Boche would realize that they had been partly deceived by the Pole, and that, in consequence, that latter would be called upon to surrender the whole of the inventor's secret. Less than three months remained, therefore, for Rouletabille to save Paris from the redoubtable *Titania*—but that lapse of time could not be guaranteed; in the last two months, events might have moved on, and reduced it considerably.

That was what it was necessary to determine, before anything else. And to find out, it was necessary to make contact with one of the three people over whose heads one of the most formidable dramas the world had ever known was being played out: Fulbert, his daughter Nicole or Serge Kaniewsky.

To make contact with them, it was necessary to discover whether all three were being held in or outside the factory, and precisely where they were, how far apart they were from one another and how far from Rouletabille.

To operate outside the factory, Rouletabille had engaged Vladimir; to operate inside, he had recruited La Candeur. Would he find those two aides at their posts? That was a second question to settle as soon as possible, for Rouletabille obviously could not work in the same way if he had a week before him rather than two months, or if he had to operate on his own rather than as a group of three.

He gave himself three days to discover the answers to those questions.

After making that resolution, fatigue seemed to overwhelm him momentarily. He fell into a semi-sleep and let his extinct pipe fall on to the floor. The noise that it made as it fell immediately woke him up. He was ashamed of himself, threw himself to the foot of his bed, reached down to pick up his pipe and suddenly stopped at the sight of an extraordinary object, which almost drew an exclamation of joy from him.

Under the bed beside his own there was a shoe—a enormous shoe! There were, in fact, two of them, the second being hidden behind the one he could see. And that shoe was sufficient for Rouletabille's happiness. Oh, that beautiful footwear! He recognized it. That lovely leather! So well cared-for, shiny and polished, magnificent! And there it was! The owner of that shoe certainly had to be something like a 47, or more!

His heart beating rapidly, Rouletabille reached out with a tremulous hand toward bed number 8 and picked up one shoe, then the other. For some time he considered that enormous pair of shoes without being able to retain a few small sighs of satisfaction.

It's him! he said to himself. *There can't be anyone but him walking around here in such superb boots!*

The reporter could no longer doubt that favorable destiny had made him La Candeur's room-mate. To be sure, Rouletabille had aided fortune somewhat with his plans, and it was perfectly normal for the Boche to aggregate in the same group the prisoners of war who were to work in the same factory; the most perfect schemes, however, are not always rewarded by such a mathematical realization. The young man's heart was warmed again. He had confidence in the imminent future.

It was about half past noon when there was a great stir in the corridor; it was the prisoners returning from work. On Sundays, the authorities granted them the entire afternoon to relax, walk in their courtyard or write. They could even play dominoes or draughts in the common room.

When the crew from his dormitory irrupted into the room, Rouletabille was lying on his bed, his eyes wide open.

Eight prisoners filed past him, wishing him an amicable bonjour while taking off their work-clothes. Some went to the bathroom; the others asked him a few questions. He replied vaguely, affecting extreme fatigue...and closed his eyes.

He had not seen La Candeur, and did not want to ask anyone any questions.

Suddenly, the floor of the corridor began to creak under powerful footfalls; Rouletabille's heart beat more precipitately, and the reporter opened his eyes again. Le Candeur came in.

La Candeur did not see Rouletabille immediately. He threw his jacket on his bed, crying: "*Oof!* That's the work's final sprint finished!" Then he let himself fall on to his bed, which creaked—after which, Le Candeur took his shoes off, repeatedly uttering "Ow!" in a lamentable fashion.

"What's wrong now, Pichenette?" asked one of the prisoners.

"Dan it, I forbid you to call me that! Do you hear, Enflé?"

"You call me Enflé, when I haven't two got sous' worth of lard beneath my skin, so I can call you Pichenette, who have a fist that could stun an ox!"

"Possibly—but I have a real name, which it's necessary not to forget. It's...René Duval. Quite simply! *Oof*—I can no longer remember it myself!" Le Candeur groaned, aside, standing up after depositing his clothes carefully at the foot of his bed. As he straightened up, he suddenly perceived Rouletabille.

At first, he quivered. His huge body oscillated like a pendulum; then his mouth opened enormously...and closed again on the exclamation, of which nothing could be heard but a distant groan.

With his fixed stare, Rouletabille left "René Duval" thunderstruck.

"Well, Pichenette," Enflé added. "What's the matter now?"

"I'm groaning at the thought of the wretched dinner we're going to have!" La Candeur replied, turning his gaze away from Rouletabille's with an effort. "They surely aren't going to serve us tripe in the Caen style."

"Would you also like a bowl of Normandy cider?"

"Alas!"

"Hang on—there's the bell!"

Two strident whistle-blasts summoned the men to table. The little dormitory emptied. La Candeur and Rouletabille were left alone there. The latter had closed his eyes again. When he reopened them he saw La Candeur contemplating him, as motionless as a statue, not daring to say a word.

"Would you like to go eat with the others, Monsieur René Duval? I don't know you, myself."

La Candeur turned and left the room, bumping into the furniture in is joy. Rouletabille had finally arrived!

La Candeur had been waiting for him for a fortnight—or, rather, was no longer hoping to see him arrive. Had not Rouletabille said to him: "I'll be in Essen before you.

The giant did not eat, and was the first to return to the dormitory.

Rouletabille turned his back on him and pretended to be fast sleep.

La Candeur uttered a sigh that would have melted the heart of a tiger. It only succeeded in getting him a sly kick in the belly from Rouletabille, who seemed to be continuing to sleep peacefully.

It was not until five o'clock, when Rouletabille was certain that no one could hear, that he permitted La Candeur to take advantage of the solitude in which the two of them had been left to relieve the pressure of his loving, devoted but unheroic heart.

In any case, the *Époque* reporter soon put a stop to the sentimental chatter and subjected La Candeur to a tightly-focused interrogation that permitted him to learn as many useful things as possible in the shortest space of time.

Thus, he learned that the prisoners of war working in the factory, and who had formerly slept in a camp outside the city, had been conclusively installed inside the factories, whose gates they would no longer go through, since the escape of two prisoner workers that had occurred a few months earlier. That way, there was no longer any indiscretion to be feared regarding the Krupp factories, for as long as the war might last.

That had resulted, moreover, in better treatment for the prisoners. They had benefited from the firmer barracks of the unmarried factory-workers, a few hundred of whom were now at the front.

These facilities, simultaneously dedicated to prisoners of war and foreign workers from neutral nations, were called *Arbeiterheime*. Prisoners and foreign workers were treated almost identically, with the same surveillance. Everywhere there were foreign workers in a factory there were sentinels with bayonets fitted to their rifles; the workers were searched as often as the prisoners, and watched as closely. A particularly high wage helped them get over these slight inconveniences.

In the *arbeiterheim* where Rouletabille and La Candeur were sleeping, there were six hundred foreign workers and a hundred French prisoners. The latter all worked in the manufacture of commercial steel or sewing-machines, the only work they could accept.

"And how many soldiers watch over an *arbeiterheim* like ours?"

"Twenty territorials, who come back with us to man our particular barracks when we're summoned to meals or to sleep, and who follow us into the different workshops where we toil, never ceasing to keep watch on us."

"Twenty! That's not many!" Rouletabille observed.

"Bah! It's too many for what they have to fear," La Candeur replied. "What do you expect anyone to do against them? Remember that they have machine-guns, and we'd be shot down in five seconds, just like that, old chap! We'd have four hundred thousand Boche workers on our backs before the general who has the responsibility of giving the order had time to telephone all the guard-rooms and rally his legion. Oh, they're sure of us! So sure that we sometime enjoy a relative freedom."

"Really? But I thought your guards never relaxed?"

"In all the workshops, while we're working—but they leave us almost in peace here. We can go down to the canteen at certain times, and by slipping out of the room one can prolong one's stay in the canteen by night, if one knows how to arrange things with Père Bachstein."

"Who's Père Bachstein?"

"That what they call him here! Father Brick—it appears that Bachstein, in German, means 'brick.' You probably knew that already."

"Oh! The *feldwebel* who oversees the floor!"

"Exactly."

"But he seems terrible!"

"He only seems it. He makes money off us, you know—he's a war profiteer! The amorous ruin themselves for him."

"The amorous?"

"Yes indeed! There are always people who need to tell stories to ladies. Our canteen-manager has two daughters as fresh as ripe wheat, who have a few friends who aren't too faded..."

"Paying court to Boche demoiselles! Do you think that's appropriate, in time of war, La Candeur?"

"It's not a matter of knowing what I think, it's a matter of knowing that for five marks, there's a *feldweg* who'll close his eyes if you're not in your bed at the exact time when the orders are to snore! That might perhaps interest you, Rouletabille, even if the canteen-manager's demoiselles don't. Because, listen carefully, it's necessary not to forget that you haven't yet explained anything to me...and I don't suppose that we're here simply to..."

He stopped, hesitating before a certain furrowing of Rouletabille's brows. Then he resumed, timidly: "You make me shiver! What's going to happen here, old chap? Now you're here! At least you aren't planning to declare war, as at the Black Castle? We can't do that here, you know. It's not just the machine-guns. There are cannons everywhere. Do you know that they're shipping cannons out of here for the navy? Cannons twelve meters long, old chap, no less! Fitting shells a meter fifty long! You can't fight cannons like that, eh?"

Impatiently, Rouletabille leaned toward La Candeur.

"You'll know everything. I've come—or, rather, we've come—to fight a cannon three hundred meters long!"

La Candeur started. "You still haven't lost the habit of making fun of folk!" he moaned.

"Quiet! Someone's coming."

And Rouletabille resumed snoring, while La Candeur polished his shoes.

Chapter XII
The Monster is There...

The night passed without incident. Rouletabille slept like a log. La Candeur, however, never closed his eyes. With Rouletabille, it was necessary to wait for everything, and La Candeur had been paid back several times over for knowing that the most extravagant—and, alas, the most dangerous—were generally those that the greatest reporter in the world attempted.

The next morning, when they left the *arbeiterheim* to go to the workshops, Rouletabille unobtrusively came to place himself beside La Candeur in the rank, and as they were allowed to talk, and the guards accompanying them were not paying any attention to them, they talked.

La Candeur told Rouletabille that the "*kommando*" of civilian and foreign industry was under the direction of a neutral who had been working at the Krupp factory for many years. That neutral was an engineer of Germanic Swiss origin, all of whose Boche relatives were working at the factory, and who had graduated from the École Polytechnique de Zurich. His name was Richter; he must have been about forty, and was about to marry the daughter of engineer Hans, the director of the Energy Laboratory. That daughter, Helena, was the niece, via her late mother, of General von Berg, who was at the head of the general *kommando*, the central directive organization of the entire factory, from the technical viewpoint.

"Everyone thinks," La Candeur explained, "that it's a case of favoring his relatives and friends and consider them as rogues for exploiting the 'war mine'—which won't have ruined everyone in the world, I can assure you."

"I see that you still like gossip, Monsieur René Duval."

"Yes, I've always had something of the concierge in me," admitted La Candeur. "It doesn't do anyone any harm, and I thought that it might be useful to you."

"And how did you learn all this?"

"Between two bouts of packing, my dear Monsieur Talmar, we chat, and Enflé, who's a packer with me, has learned a great many things, because he knows German."

"You're a packer, then? What do you pack?"

"Sewing-machines, of course! I'm the one who supervises the packing on Sundays, when there's nothing else left to do but put the machines in the boxes. During the week I work in the distribution of the primary components. Basically, they've made me a porter, and I quite like that—it permits me to get around. At first they put me to manufacturing control-levers and shuttles, but the work was too delicate; I was too clumsy and broke too many. There was a reason for that! I was afraid that they'd perceive my inexperience and I told them right away that I did heavy work at the factory that employed me. It's worked out, as you can see."

"Yes, not too badly. So, you told me that the packers can chat a little between themselves? What else do they say?"

"Aha—you're getting a taste for conversation. Well, know that there are a few *sozialdemocrates* here with whom one can chat if one knows the language. Enflé's's talked to a few of them. That's how I learned that Krupp's has, it seems, an occult administration of control and reciprocal surveillance between all the chiefs, like the one that's said to exist in the Jesuit Order. Each of them is suspicious of the others and thinks he sees spies everywhere. They make alliances, conspire, hatch plots and betray one another. People are always talking about their organization. It's possible, but some chiefs, it seems, are most expert in organizing pilfering. You can well imagine that there must be a lot of pilfering in a business like this. When I see all the things that are manufactured here, you know, I can't help smiling at the idea that anyone thought that they'd run out of munitions after six months of war!"

In fact, during that journey through the factory, necessarily slow because of the obstacles encountered at every moment, it was possible to take account of the formidable supply of raw materials, their rapid transformation into projectiles of all kinds and weapons of every caliber.

Trains were gliding incessantly in every direction, bringing in iron and steel, taking out cannon and mortars, in an atmosphere that was thick and hot and asphyxiating, behind locomotives vomiting black smoke, amid the tramp of thousands upon thousands of workers, who had barely had time to sleep before retaking their places before the furnaces, from which the night shifts were fleeing with ghostly faces.

A nudge of La Candeur's elbow made Rouletabille turn round.

"Look!—here, this building…it's the munitions depot for the 420s. Look—there are more shells arriving. Isn't it frightful? They never stop making them, you know. You were joking yesterday with your 300-meter cannon…"

A sharp kick from Rouletabille on La Candeur's enormous boot made the giant grimace, amazed to see his companion's distressed face.

"I forbid you, you hear, ever to mention that cannon again!" Rouletabille hissed between his teeth. "I forbid it—on pain of death!" And as La Candeur, pale and frightened, no longer knew where he was, he added: "But go on then, idiot! You were saying that they had depots..."

"Yes, an ammunition depot for every caliber," poor La Candeur stammered, increasingly bewildered. "There's one for 77s, 120s, 105s, 150s, 210s, 420s, 280s, 350s, and you've just seen the one for 420s."

"It was said that they were running short of 420s..."

"I don't care—even if they have none for the moment, they're making seven at a time in the foundry. So...hang on, look over there!"

"Ah! God, that's worth the trouble of getting out of bed," said Rouletabille, considering two prodigious containers that had just appeared to their left, between the countless iron pillars that surrounded them. They were two enormous Krupp gas reservoirs, the largest in the world.

"And they're always full to bursting, you know! Just think! With one bomb from an airplane over-head...what a bang!"

"Shut up, I tell you—shut up!"

It was La Candeur's turn to observe Rouletabille's pallor. The latter was no longer looking at the reservoirs, but beyond their formidable rotundity, at something even more formidable.

In the smoky atmosphere, torn by a sudden gust of wind, a nightmarish monument, which seemed to be built on hellish clouds, raised up its colossal silhouette.

It was really there: the hideous and terrible carapace of the war-machine, which Nourry had evoked before dying. Rouletabille recognized its fantastic dimensions and the inclination, inexplicable at first glance, of its gigantic roof, which was much higher at the southern end than the northern end—and, finally, Rouletabille recognized the orientation of the monster: north-east/south-west; the direction of Paris.

"Oh, you're looking at the hangar of their new Zeppelin," whispered La Candeur. "It appears that it's a new model, more marvelous than all the rest. Yes, a new invention of a Polish engineer who's found a means of transporting a veritable fortress through the air. Can you believe how stubborn they are, with their Zeppelins. They lose them all the time; it's necessary to reconstruct them all the time—and bigger and bigger ones. That one will be in the three hundred met..."

Another terrible kick on La Candeur's shoe brought a dull exclamation from the poor fellow.

"I forbid it, you hear!" Rouletabille hissed again, his eyes flashing. "I forbid you to pronounce that figure!"

"All right, all right," the other sighed. "Understood. All the more so as I'll end up with corns on my feet if I go on."

Nothing could be seen of the building but its superstructure. As Nourry had said, it was oddly positioned between workshops, some of which had been half-demolished to "let it pass." The whole edifice was surrounded by a high and interminable wall of planks, guarded by a cordon of troops.

"Can you believe that they're taking such precautions? It's said that special workers are working there, under special surveillance. It's also said that their new

Zeppelin will soon be ready," La Candeur added. "We'll soon see what it is—personally, I'm in no hurry. It's probably one of those defective dodges with which they're always trying to bluff the world. But what's the matter with you, old chap? You look as if something..."

Rouletabille's ears were ringing furiously then, not only because they had been painfully struck by the remark that "it's said that their new Zeppelin will soon be ready," but also because he could hear, all along the wall of planks that the prisoners were following behind their guardians, the innumerable echoes of the work that was going on behind it.

A tumult of motors and hammers gave a terrible sensation of the haste with which a population of workers was rushing joyfully and furiously to finish a gigantic task. Every impact broke the reporter's heart. *Will I still have time?* he asked himself, his entire body quivering with emotion.

Chapter XIII
Rouletabille Works Hard

Rouletabille succeeded in mastering himself, however, and resolved not to be excited or astonished by anything else until he had triumphed. He listened more attentively to La Candeur's explanations. A few minutes later, the giant pointed out more buildings to him. "That's our factory. Look—everything that you can see there is Richter's *kommando*."

Then suddenly, La Candeur said: "Well, old chap, she's early today."

"Who?"

"Can't you see her? There in the little auto that's stopping outside Richter's door. The *fräulein* on the right, in the driver's seat—that's his fiancée."

"Oh yes, Helena. She's pretty."

"I'll say. But I prefer the friend who's with her, she's less flaxen—there's no accounting for taste, you know. The other's almost chestnut. She's more like the girls back home, you might say."

In a changed voice, in spite of having sworn not to be excited by anything else, Rouletabille said: "You...don't know who her friend is?"

"Honestly, no! It's not the first time I've seen her with Helena Hans. Helena comes to see Richter almost every day. It's a friend who must live with her in the factory, or they wouldn't be seen so often together."

"And when they come together, is that orderly who's standing with his arms folded behind the car always with them?"

107

"Yes, always. He must be the chauffeur—but Helena always drives. Look—they're both getting out and going into Richter's."

"Yes, and the orderly's going with them. You can see that he's not a chauffeur."

"Possibly. Does that interest you?"

"Me? Not in the least."

Rouletabille's eyes devoured the feminine silhouette that was disappearing though Richter's doorway between Helena and the orderly. He had recognized Nicole Fulbert.

Yes, it was definitely Nicole, as he had seen her in photographs lent to him by her mother, and as she had been described to him, with her curvaceous stature, her chestnut-colored hair with coppery gleams, her lovely face, always looking down slightly, her bony and slender profile, her large dark blue eyes. Her entire physiognomy gave a strange impression of hostile melancholy...

"We've arrived," said La Candeur.

Indeed, they were going into a large courtyard surrounded by workshops. The workshops were divided into three sections. In the first the heavier components were manufactured: platforms, pedals, levers, axle-trees, flywheels, cylinders, etc. In the second the more delicate components were made: fabric-grips, bobbins, needles, hand-controls, shuttles and even springs. In the third the machines were assembled and finished off. The whole was disposed around a vast courtyard at the back of which were the storage and packing facilities.

Access to this sewing-machine section was obtained via a vast double door, through which all the merchandise went in and came out. At the back of the courtyard there was a small door connecting directly with the buildings of the commando directed by engineer Richter.

That was where the latter had his offices, in the middle of a veritable factory devoted almost exclusively to external commerce and foreign exchange.

As soon as they were inside the enclosure, Rouletabille and the other newly-arrived prisoners were subjected to a regulation interrogation by a military foreman, after which the reporter and two of his companions were taken into the engineer's offices.

They waited there for about ten minutes, and then the reporter was able to take account of the reason for the delay. Through the windows of the room to which they had been taken, he saw Helena appear on the steps of the building, then her companion, then the man who was surely charged with watching Nicole, and finally a man who might have been about forty, rather fat but handsome nevertheless because he was tall. He had to be a solid trencherman and a keen beer-drinker. He had a full blond beard, carefully groomed, and an expansive, highly intelligent face illuminated by two small and piercing gray eyes, which were presently smiling at Helena, whom he accompanied to the automobile. He shook hands with the two young women.

Rouletabille had only darted a glance at the man he assumed to be Richter, all his attention being focused on Nicole. There was no longer any room for doubt; it was definitely Fulbert's daughter. The unfortunate young woman seemed to have suffered a great deal, and seemed indifferent to everything.

The auto drew away gently, and the man came back into the offices. Two minutes later, he began interrogating the prisoners. It was indeed Richter. Rouletabille's two companions were rapidly dispatched and headed for the workshops. When the reporter's turn came, the engineer instructed a secretary to pass him the Blin & Co.

file. The employee unlocked a vast filing-cabinet and search through the files arranged there in alphabetical order.

When Richter had the file he opened a door and invited Rouletabille to go through it ahead of him. They went along a corridor and into a large empty room occupied by three large trestle-tables. The tables were strewn with blueprints, machine diagrams and so on. Richter at down on one of the high stools that were distributed around the tables, riffled through the Blin & Co. file momentarily, lingered over the reading of some kind of report, and then turned back to Rouletabille.

"Michel Talmar, you graduated from the École des Arts et Métiers. You were employed by Blin & Co. for five years. You're a hard worker of remarkable intelligence. In the different workshops through which you passed, you found the opportunity and means to introduce improvements, not only with respect to the work but from the mechanical viewpoint. When the war broke out, you were working at Blin's, in the greatest secrecy, in drawing up plans for a new sewing-machine, for which you got the idea during a trip you undertook to America in 1907. Blin's had high hopes for that machine, which would have deployed fifty needles..."

"Seventy-five," Rouletabille put in.

"Possibly. The secret was well-guarded—to the extent, at least, that it could be. Do you have a contract with Blin's?"

"No, Monsieur, not yet. It was after examining the plans that I was in the process of drawing up when the war broke out that Blin & Co. were going to make me a firm offer."

"Can you tell me something about your new machine? You understand that I'm interested. After all, you're not bound in any fashion to Blin's, and it's a Swiss engineer who's speaking to you."

"Who works for Germany."

"And who corresponds with all the world's the leading sewing-machine manufacturers. While staying here I can set you up magnificently somewhere else. Except that it's necessary for me to have some idea, not of the secret of your invention, but of the return one might hope for, the result that you propose to achieve. Anyway, I repeat, can you tell me something about it?"

Rouletabille maintained a meditative silence.

In order to stimulate him, the other said: "The mechanisms of machines are quite variable, when one moves from one model to another, but the principle remains the same, and I don't think, in any case, that you can bring a veritable revolution to that mechanism, already so refined..."

"Yes I can!" replied Rouletabille, dryly.

"You astonish me!" Richter said, swaying on his stool, with his hands clasped on his knee. "Let's see: the general functions of a sewing-machine can be divided into three movements. The first is the movement by which the needle plunges into the fabric, drawing the thread in order to seal the loop through which the shuttle will pass. The second is the movement that passes the shuttle or a circular hook through the loop formed by the thread on the needle. The third is the movement displacing the fabric after each stitch, which, in consequence, varies with the length of the stitch. The last movement is called the traction. These three movements are indispensable. They exist in all machines, varying according to the taste and ingenuity of the inventors, and when they're produced appropriately, all machines sew well if the tensions of the thread, the needle and the shuttle are well-regulated. You can still tell me which of these three movements, in addition to the extraordinary establishment of your seventy-five needles, carries your...improvement."

"I don't see any inconvenience, Monsieur, in telling you that my machine takes over those three movements, and that the improvement, as you put it, of the three movements is such that it transforms them completely. You have, of course, seen twenty-five-needle machines; mine, which has seventy-five, and can sew fabrics, hats, leather goods etc., has nothing in common, I can sure you, with those twenty-fives. Its work is unprecedented, and the parallelism between garments is perfect."

"Yes, but is it always good? In twenty-five-needle machines, for instance, when a thread breaks, the operation continues, and repairs have then to be made on a ordinary machine. With seventy-five needles, I imagine that thread-breakages..."

"With my machine," Rouletabille put in, curtly, seemingly becoming increasingly excited, "broken threads are of no importance. In your machines, you have a component that forms a knot every eight stitches, in such a way that when the thread breaks, the work is only faulty over the length of those eight stitches. My machine makes a knot at every stitch—and every needle works more rapidly than a needle on one of your machines."

"Damn!" Richter exclaimed, getting down from his stool and lighting a cigarette. "That is indeed a revolution. Do you smoke, Monsieur?"

"A pipe," said Rouletabille. "If you'll permit..."

"Please do. And would it be indiscreet to ask you what the Blins have offered you for..."

"Not at all! Fifty thousand francs on adoption of my plans, and twenty per cent of the profits."

"Would you like a light?"

"Thanks, but I have my lighter."

"Monsieur Talmar, I'm delighted to have made your acquaintance."

"Me too, Monsieur."

"Monsieur Talmar, you're not familiar with the Krupp factory?"

"No—regrettably."

"Well, permit me to give you a little tour of the factory you'd like to know about. It happens that I need to go to the *generalkommando* this morning."

The two men looked at one another momentarily, in silence. They had reached an understanding.

"You'll permit me to give a few orders? I understand from your file that you speak German."

"Yes, Monsieur..."

"I'm going to telephone for a guard to be put at your disposal. It's the regulation. You can't go out without a guard. Excuse me..."

Five minutes later, they were both traversing the factory, with the guard behind them. The engineer gave Rouletabille details of everything they passed *en route* is a very amiable fashion. He spoke about the factory with great enthusiasm.

"As regards the *generalkommando*," he told him, "it's an unparalleled managerial organization specially dedicated, in the first place, to the foundry, comprising officers from the general staff or the artillery, commanded by a general, all expert in matters of the manufacture of shells and canon. They're the one who carry out all the experiments and field-trials, and also work tirelessly in the improvement of the materiel, on new discoveries that might be useful to national defense. The services rendered to the war industry by that small nucleus of men are simply staggering. Everything is their work: new cannon, new shells, new kinds of steel, new trench-digging equipment, everything! Now, they're going to annex to the service inventions of every sort that, outside the foundry, might modify the work of the factory for purely industrial and commercial production."

"What's that enormous tower?" asked Rouletabille, without seeming to attach any particular importance to the last sentence that Richter had pronounced, with an evident purpose and while looking at him from the corner of his eye.

"That's our water-tower. Do you know that, before the war, the annual consumption of water for the Essen steelworks alone surpassed that of the city of Dresden by 225,000 cubic meters. The total figure was fourteen and a half million cubic meters a year. The network of water-pipes comprises 222 kilometers of underground distribution and 143 kilometers interior distribution. Since the war began, the length of the piping has more than tripled. That tells you how important the role played by our water-tower is."

"I've never seen one as high."

"It's sixty meters from the base to the lantern! Would you like to go up? From there you can see the entire factory, with its new annexes, and a considerable part of the city of Essen. The view is unique, and the weather is superb today!"

Rouletabille darted a glanced at his watch, which had been taken off him at Rastatt and returned to him when he left for Essen.

"I'd certainly like that," he said, "but let's go to your meeting first, because I don't want to put you out.

114

We can undertake he ascension in question on the way back from the *generalkommando*."

"As you wish."

Almost immediately, Rouletabille saw Richter bow profoundly before a superior officer, who was chatting at a window with a young woman, who raised her head precipitately and sent the engineer her most gracious smile. The reporter recognized Helena—and, half-hidden behind her, the silhouette of Nicole.

It's true that they're never apart, he thought. *They must live together...*

"Before the war," Richter said, "this was the home of the director of our Energy Laboratory, and the commandant who just saluted us is none other than the director himself, the famous engineer Hans. And look, over there, the building with the three characteristic chimneys—that's the Energy Laboratory itself. At this moment, there's some very interesting work on radium going on there..."

In the meantime, Richter and Helena had not stopped smiling at one another in the most amiable fashion.

My opinion, Rouletabille thought, thanking Providence for having caused him to fall upon a Swiss engineer in love, *is that the excellent Monsieur Richter took us on a little detour via the water tower in order to have an opportunity to see his beauty again! I don't have any complaint!*

Whatever happened at the *generalkommando* was quite rapid. Rouletabille was left in a small waiting-room with his guard, who had never ceased to follow him. Ten minutes went by; then Richter came to find our hero and took him into an office where he found himself confronted by two highly-placed individuals whom he subsequently discovered to be General von Berg and the chief engineer to inventions for internal and external commerce and industry. He was asked to repeat what he had already said about his machine, rather brutally, or at least in terms that were intended to disturb him and make him understand that he would not be permitted to keep his secret to himself for very long.

He thought it as well to march in the same direction as the gentlemen in question, and started blushing and stammering in a natural manner that would have delighted La Candeur.

He repeated everything they wanted to hear.

Finally, the chief engineer said to him: "Herr Richter, who is a Swiss subject, has asked us to make you the following offer: two hundred thousand francs on the admission of your plans and thirty per cent of the profits. Think about it! Blin are robbing you! We've known Herr Richter for fifteen years. He's an honest man. Go!"

Richter and Rouletabille went out of the *generalkommando*, still followed by the soldier.

Richter seemed to have completely forgotten the conversation they had just had at the *kommando*, but he did not forget to go past the Energy Laboratory again, and the house where Hans and his daughter lived. This time, however, they did not have the pleasure of seeing Helena.

When they reached the water-tower, Rouletabille looked at his watch again. "Shall we go up?" he asked.

"At your disposal," said Richter.

They went up. The tower was octagonal in shape, and Richter explained as they climbed that its summit enclosed a reservoir of 150 tons. The water, which was brought to the foot of the tower by six-kilometer channels, came from the great artificial lake formed by the exhaustion of the coal mines in the Ruhr basin. Steam-pumps raised the water within the tower and, once in the reservoir, it was propelled by its own weight in all directions within the factory.

Rouletabille and Richter arrived at the tower's lantern a trifle breathless. The weather was fine, but the horizon was as hazy as that of the sea.

As Rouletabille gazed into the distance, Richter said to him: "The interest isn't a long way off, or even in front of you—it's at you feet. You only have to look down to embrace with a single glance this world of factories, from which the German Empire has emerged as if from an infernal cavern, and with which it now faces up to the entire world. What strikes you first is the surrounding railway, traced like a magic circle around the factory of the hundred gates! It projects a vast radiance of tracks in every direction. Those buildings that extend in the direction of the city are workshops for the manufacture of canon."

"What's that noise?" Rouletabille inquired. "Are they conducting trials?"

"No, that's the big fifty-thousand-kilogram hammer at work. It cost two and a half million. It's supported by three gigantic foundations, one in stone one in oak-trunks from the forest of Teutoburg, and another in bronze, formed of solidly-linked cylinders. It forges four-hundred-quintal blocks! That's common knowledge."

Rouletabille allowed himself to be guided around the lantern. Eventually, he asked, casually: "But what's that enormous and bizarre construction, which has such a curious roof? We went past it this morning."

"That's the cradle of our new Zeppelin," Richter replied. "Something astonishing, it seems—but between

117

us, it's better not to talk about it, in order not to have any disagreements with the administration, which knows everything that happens here, and everything that's said."

"Bah!"

"Oh, I'd rather you took notice! The police are very efficient!"

"I don't doubt it," Rouletabille said, indifferently. "And down there, in the town, facing us, in the direction of that steeple—what's that magnificent house?"

"Oh, that's the factory's house. It's the Essener-Hoff. That's where Herr Krupp lodges his friends and receives his crowned guests. Kaiser Wilhelm often spends a day or two there. Trials are carried out before him then, on the firing-range hidden by that roof, which extends all the way to the horizon, of new items of artillery whose existence is kept secret..."

Rouletabille no longer seemed to be following Richter's explanations, and the latter finally noticed it.

"What are you looking at in that fashion?" he asked.

"The Essener-Hoff, which you showed me just now. It's extraordinary what you can see from here. Look—there are people on the balcony. It would be wonderful, wouldn't it, if that were the Emperor?"

Richter started laughing.

"Why not? You said that he comes here some-times..."

Still laughing, Richter knocked on the door of a small cabin adjacent to the lantern. The door opened and a man appeared, clad in a special tunic and wearing a red cap, of a type that Rouletabille had already noticed during his morning perambulations. Richter asked the man for a pair of prismatic binoculars, which he aimed at the place indicated by his new employee, the balcony of the Essener-Hoff.

"No, no, it's not the Emperor. See for yourself,"

Rouletabille looked, and almost immediately handed the binoculars back to the engineer. "No, it's not the Emperor; he doesn't resemble his portraits," he said, laughing in his turn. And he added, privately: *It's not him because it's Vladimir Féodorovitch, faithfully manning his post, at the appointed hour, on the balcony of the Essener-Hoff, waiting for a message to fall from the sky sent by Rouletabille. He's arrived! That's all I wanted to know...*

Turning to Richter, who was already preparing to go down, he said: "Who is the man in the tunic and red cap in the cabin?"

"He's the duty fireman," the engineer replied. "He's the one who raises the first alarm as soon as a fire starts. He's in communication by telephone and also by means of luminous signals with the entire factory."

"What organization! It's marvelous!"

"And to think that it all came out of that little thing you can see down there," said the engineer. "That poor little forge near the main gate! It was in there that Krupp senior, himself just a simple and wretched worker, worked for a long time beside his own father, who was merely a poor blacksmith, who sold the various objects he made personally, in the vicinity. It's understandable that the son was determined to preserve that curious and precious testimony to the humble origins of one of the most powerful organizations in the world."

Emerging from the tower, the two men did not say anything further until they had returned to the engineer's design-studio. There, as Richter was still silent, Rouletabille—who had assumed a rather preoccupied expression, finally said: "Listen, Monsieur, I've thought about it. I accept the proposal you made to me. There's no reason why I should refuse to deal with a Swiss engineer. I'm not, in fact, bound in any fashion to Blin & Co., who have only made me vague promises, which are, in any case, much less generous than yours. You can, therefore, draw up our contract, and I'll set to work myself, if you give me the means, on drawing up the plans."

Richter held out his hand and Rouletabille shook it.

"It's agreed, then," the engineer concluded. "And you can see that I'm delighted, for myself and for you. You've made a good decision. Personally, I wouldn't have mentioned it to you again. We don't intend to force anyone, but we know how to reward those who are willing. You'll see. You won't have any regrets."

Then he headed for a small room that formed an annex to the design studio, and which had only one door—the one communicating with the studio. It served, at present, as a cloakroom and lumber-room. A large window poured daylight on to a large table raised on trestles, which as designed for drawing standing up.

"You'll be right at home here," said Richter, "and never disturbed. No one in fact, comes into my design-studio unless I introduce them myself. You can start work today!"

That evening, when Rouletabille found himself alone with La Candeur momentarily in the dormitory and the latter asked him whether he was content with his day, the reporter said: "Yes, I've worked hard."

He had good reason to be satisfied. He had given himself three days to resolve two primordial problems. Already, he knew that he could count on La Candeur and Vladimir; he had familiarized himself with the general layout of the factory, including the place where the *Titania* was under construction—and where, in consequence, the Pole was—the Energy Laboratory, where Fulbert was working, and the home of the engineer Hans, where Nicole must be living. He had seen Nicole. He was in Richter's good graces and was working in his offices, where Nicole sometimes came with Helena, Hans's daughter. And he still had two days left to find out how much more time he had to save Paris from the terrible *Titania*.

Chapter XIV
A Dramatic Interview

It was not by chance that Rouletabille had assumed the identity of Michel Talmar of Blin & Co. Talmar, who had been apprised of what Rouletabille had come to look for in his workshops, had needed no further recommendation to give the reporter his own papers and to help him study in depth the plans of an invention whose secret the Boche had already attempted to discover in peace-time.

Everything was going as well as could be desired for Rouletabille, who had naturally promised Talmar only to surrender those of his plans that would be useful for his own enterprise—and the day after the one on which the reporter had accepted the Swiss engineer's offer, we find him in the process of tracing the first lines of an important diagram under Richter's eyes, in the small room reserved for him.

The noise of an automobile drawing to a halt at the front door attracted the attention of both men. Richter immediately left Rouletabille. Through the window, the latter perceived Helena, who got out of the car and came into the office building.

In the next room there was a rapid conversation between Helena and Richter, in which there was some discussion of a sumptuous engagement party to be held in a few days time at the Essener-Hoff, under the presidency of General von Berg, the director of the *generalkomando* and uncle of the bride-to-be. That important relationship ought to give the party an exceptional luster, and the representatives of the allied States who were guests at the Essener-Hoff involved in dealings with General von Berg would be invited to it. Then a few words were exchanged in low voices, in which the names of Nicole and Fulbert were discernible, and the words "the Emperor's will!"

Finally there were some perfectly clear sentences: "No! I haven't brought Nicole out today. Before going back to the commando, the general wanted to see her in private. I think there's something new in the air!"

One can easily imagine the interest with which Rouletabille listened to what was being said on the other side of his door, and how much he regretted that Nicole had not come with Helena.

The next day, however, the two young women arrived together, still followed by the obligatory guard, who waited for them in the vestibule. The man in question wore a special uniform, half military and half resembling that of a domestic in an aristocratic household, and one could take one's choice as to whether to think of him as an orderly or a butler. Rouletabille learned subsequently that the factory administration had a certain number of domestic staff of that sort, who were put at the disposal of important people from abroad visiting Essen, and whose fundamental role was to keep them under assiduous surveillance. They belonged to the secret police that La Candeur had mentioned.

Helena and Nicole had, as was their habit, come into the engineer's private design-studio, and the latter soon made a precipitate entrance behind them. The first thing he did was go to the door of the little room where Rouletabille was working. He looked inside and saw that it was empty. The reporter, in fact, had just hurled himself into a cupboard in which draughtsman' smocks were hanging.

Richter closed the door again, satisfied, and the following scene unfolded. It was to have such important consequences for the remainder of the story that we think it best to reproduce here the text in which Rouletabille described its rapid developments himself.

"I understood immediately," the reporter wrote, "on perceiving Mademoiselle Fulbert's strangely distressed face through the window of my workroom, that there must indeed be something new in her respect, as Fräulein Hans had said the day before—and that my good fortune and the successful outcome of my plans would doubtless permit me to witness and event of the greatest interest for my mission in Essen.

"When the young women were in the room adjacent to my office and I heard the hurried footsteps of the engineer heading for my door, I did not hesitate to hide and had the joy of seeing the door close again, in the conviction that the room was empty. Richter must have thought that I was busy in workshop number 3, where I had to copy a number of prototypes, in order to establish the difference, from certain technical viewpoints, between them and my own model—with the result that I could hear in total security what was happening in the next room, and even catch a glimpse from time to time, through the keyhole, of the characters in the drama.

"Richter was striding back and forth, quite agitated. With regard to the two young women, who were sitting on the far side of the room, I only had a clear view of Nicole's face, which was reflecting the most hostile sentiments at that moment. Until then, I had been primarily struck by an appearance of pain, but that day it expressed a concentrated fury against her torturers. To judge by what I could see, the poor child must have suffered greatly and she seemed to be at the end of her tether.

"'Mademoiselle,' Richter said to her, 'you know how much Helena loves you. She treats you like a sister. If you're not more cheerful or healthier, it's not her fault. Helena has told you that you're about to find yourself in the presence of Serge Kaniewsky. I shall be particularly grateful to you if you do not conceal from him the care and affection that has been lavished upon you. You are not among enemies here, as you know very well, and I have always has the greatest sympathy for your misfortunes. You're on neutral ground here, among friends. I hope that you similarly appreciate the delicacy of the procedure in high places that has resulted in my house being chosen for an interview that has been granted to the insistent pleas of your fiancé. You have every facility and liberty to exchange with him the words that are dear to two individuals who love one another—but for the very reason that you are on neutral terrain, you will easily understand that it will be impossible to tolerate the slightest allusion to subjects that have any relationship whatsoever to the war. I'm sure, Mademoiselle, that you have understood me, and that I shall not have to repent of the generosity that Helena and I have always manifested toward you.'

"After which, there was a silence; and the Helena' voice was heard.

"'Be reasonable, Nicole, won't you? Answer us, Nicole. It's necessary. It's necessary, for all our sakes...who are so afraid for you. It's necessary, for your father's sake. It's necessary, for your fiancé. What is it that we're asking of you? To tell Serge that we're treating you like a friend and that we're caring for you with all our hearts. It's not difficult to say such a thing, which is true and will give us pleasure! We're not asking anything else of you!'

"But Nicole still remained silent. Her beautiful face, ordinarily downcast, was, however upraised—but that movement was far from giving more mildness to her distraught physiognomy.

"At this point a general came in, whom I assumed to be General von Berg in person, and a man who passed through my field of vision and who immediately seemed to me to be in a state of extreme physical and moral distress. I had no difficulty in understanding that I had the Pole before me, given the first movement he made on perceiving Nicole. He threw himself at her feet. At the same time, the general made a sign to Richter and Helena, and the latter two left the room.

"Nicole had pulled back her chair before Serge's movement, but he continued to drag himself toward her on his knees, without hearing the rude objurgations of von Berg, who told him to be reasonable if he wanted this interview with his fiancée to be followed by any others. The other did nothing but weep and moan, however, and beg for forgiveness. He tried to embrace Nicole's feet and kiss the hem of her skirt, and begged her to tell him that she still loved him—but Nicole did not reply, and her face became increasingly harsh.

"For myself—this is Rouletabille speaking—I could not help wondering, confronted by that double attitude, whether there might be a considerable component of play-acting within it, designed to persuade the Boche general that he had not been deceived, and that the factory possessed the whole secret of the *Titania*. There must certainly have been something of that sort, but I was also obliged to yield to the evidence that Nicole's hostility was too real to be addressed to a man who had only put

126

on a semblance of betraying her. She certainly saw a man whom she knew to be capable of betraying her, and was still ready to betray anything for love of her!

"That Serge was ready to do that, I could no more doubt than Nicole herself or Fulbert—remember what he had told Malet, as reported by Nourry—and that was my thinking because the sincere tears that the Pole was shedding at present, and his unfeigned despair, could not relate to a false crime in the past, while they were perfectly consonant with a true crime that he was yet to commit.

"In consequence of that, although the general might have been mistaken with regard to the meaning of the forgiveness demanded by the Pole from his fiancée, neither Nicole nor I was deceived. Serge was about to commit the real treason, and would do so!

"Still from my own viewpoint—I am obliged to follow my reasoning step by step here—the unusual mental disturbance of which the Pole was giving proof attested that the moment when all would be revealed—that is to say, when he would be obliged to betray it in order to save Nicole—could not be very far off, for such an excess would not be comprehensible if the Pole still intended to continue lying for months.

"The Pole was weeping so helplessly, and Nicole's face had hardened to such an extent, that General von Berg rapidly came to the conclusion that the conference had lasted long enough. He dragged Serge to his feet, taking hold of him by the collar of his jacket, and said: 'I promised that you could see Mademoiselle Fulbert! You've seen her! You've been able to observe that Mademoiselle Fulbert is perfectly well, and she'll tell you herself that she's being looked after like a sister by Mademoiselle Hans. Isn't that so, Mademoiselle? In truth, it's you duty to say so!'

"But Nicole continued to say nothing at all.

"Then Serge fell to his knees, like the madman he was. 'So you won't take pity on your Serge!' he croaked. "Say something! Answer me! Answer him! Tell me that you're being cared for. Tell me that you're no longer suffering. Oh, Nicole, tell me that you're no longer suffering! I don't want you to suffer any more! You'll detest me, you'll curse me, but you won't be suffering anymore! I don't want anyone to hurt you. No, no…I don't want that! I wasn't able to resist such a thing, you see— your torture, my Nicole, tortured! Oh, rather the end of the world! The end of the world! What it is that makes my world? What is it that makes my Paris and all the cities in the world? I can't see you any more as I saw you before, on a wretched bed in a dungeon, I can't hear you sighing in pain any longer. My Nicole, my Nicole! Say something! Go on, curse me! At least I'll hear the sound of your voice! If you knew, if you only knew! They showed me photographs, the monsters! Atrocious photographs of poor Russian prisoners they tortured in Poland. Broken limbs…breasts torn with red-hot pincers! All the horrors of the Inferno! And they told me that all of that was in store for you! Understand then! I couldn't! I can't! I can't! My God, I can't! No, no…!'

"And the poor fellow, in a frightful crisis, having been pushed away by Nicole's foot, stood up, tottering, and showed me his demonic face, which I hadn't yet glimpsed. A frightful vision! Hideousness and dolor combined to make that mask the most tragic and most frightful thing to behold that can be imagined.

"Oh, how ugly that man was! And how he was suffering! How pitiful he seemed! Al my life I shall have the awful contraction of that horrible and magnificent hideousness in my eyes. All my life, I shall have those lamentable tears and desperate groans in my ears!

"He stood up straight, tearing at his hair and crying: 'If only I could die! But I can't die! Yes, they've even made certain of that! Death itself is forbidden me. Death doesn't want me! You don't know, you don't know that if I die before having brought their accursed work to completion, they've promised to burn you with small fires—small fires, do you hear?'

"At that point, he uttered a frightful laugh, and suddenly, I had the terror, in the face of such despair and such a semblance of madness, that he had already talked, that he had given up everything, said everything: a sensation that made my limbs grow weak and made me hold on, breathlessly to that door, behind which the greatest drama on earth was unfolding—a further stage in my reasoning, a further illumination of my inflamed brain—and that sensation, I immediately thought, Nicole must have experienced simultaneously, for she, whose voice I had not yet heard, suddenly raised herself up in the most passionate movement and howled at him: 'A thousand deaths! A thousand deaths! For me and for you and for my father, rather than your crime!'

"And she tried to grab hold of him, in order to howl again: 'I'll let myself die of starvation! I'll let myself go!'

"She did not have the time to continue, though; General von Berg, who had doubtless had his reasons for letting the Pole's despair overflow, had rushed upon Nicole as soon as he had heard her, and, with an indescribable brutality, dragged her all the way to my door and threw her into the little room where I had taken refuge, which he naturally assumed to be empty.

"I only just had time to flatten myself against the wall. He didn't see me, and locked the door with the key.

"At that moment, I heard him shouting for the guard, who was in the vestibule, to whom he gave an order to remain in front of the door, and he went away with the Pole, who filled the house with his demented screams.

"As for me, I was already bending down over Nicole's recumbent body. She was semi-conscious, but I soon brought her back to her senses by saying to her: 'I've come here to save you. I've seen your mother. I've been sent here by the French government, to save you and to save Paris from the *Titania*!'

She stood up as if moved by a spring, then looked me straight in the eyes with her somber and steely gaze. 'There's only one way to save us all,' she whispered, 'and that's to kill me!' When I'm dead, the other won't say anything more, because he'll no longer have to fear that they'll make me suffer! So kill me, Monsieur! If you have a weapon, kill me, and I'll be saved! I've tried myself, several times, but they watch me. They never leave me. At night, in my room, there's always an old woman who never closes her eyes. They force-feed me when I refuse to eat. For God's sake, if there's no weapon here, there're must be a nail from which to hang me. Hurry, for they won't leave me alone for long.'

"I had all the difficulty in the world stopping her speaking, from raving deliriously, but my hand over her mouth stifled her, crushing half of her insane words. Finally, I was able to master her. 'Do you think he's given up the secret of the compensating rudder?' I asked.

"She recovered her self-composure then. 'No, but it's as good as done. You heard the poor madman! When the moment comes, he won't hold out against them.'

"'If he hasn't talked yet, nothing's lost yet,' I said.

"'But he will talk! He will talk! Didn't you understand that in his delirium?'

"'Yes, but how much time is there before he has to talk?'

"'He'll have to talk on the twenty-first of the month, and it's now the sixth. He'll have to talk in a fortnight.'

"Suffocated by those figures, which I was far from expecting, stammered: 'But it isn't possible that they've had time to build the *Titania*...'"

"She interrupted me: 'Certainly! Not the big *Titania*, which won't be finished for three months, but it's a matter of the scale model that they've decided to construct in parallel with the big *Titania* and which will be ready for testing in a fortnight—and perhaps Serge will talk even before then. There's no longer any hope, I tell you! I know Serge. His love for me extends to the mot somber madness, and is nourished by the hatred he has for the rest of the human race. We're doomed, I tell you, if you don't kill me!'

"'Mademoiselle,' I declared, then, "I swear to you, personally, that if I have not saved you all within a fortnight, then I will kill you, with this hand, which won't tremble. And I assure you that I will find a means to reach Serge Kaniewsky thereafter, to say to him: *She died in order that you wouldn't talk.*'

"And that admirable young woman looked me straight in the eyes and said: 'Do one of those two things—save us or kill me—and you will be blessed.'

"With that, she made the sign of the cross—but I had grabbed a piece of paper and a pencil, and I said to her: 'Write this: *My beloved Serge, I died in order that you wouldn't talk.*'

"She wrote it in a firm hand and signed it. I put the piece of paper in my pocket.

"'What's your name?' she asked, still in a low voice.

"I relied: 'My name is Michel Talmar so far as everyone here is concerned, but for you, I'm Rouletabille,'

"Then I heard the door open. It was General Berg, engineer Richter, engineer Hans and his daughter, coming in search of Nicole. I threw myself into my hiding-place. As for her, she prepared to go with them quietly—but she didn't have the strength, and they had to carry her away."

Chapter XV
A Night in Hell

Three days have passed since the last scene. It is midnight. The prodigious forge is working as in broad daylight. By virtue of what habituation, what rapid education, can human beings sleep in the midst of the formidable resonance of that labor of giants?

In the immense barracks of workers and prisoners known as *arbeiterheime*, the day-shift workers are nevertheless asleep, exhausted.

It is probable that Rouletabille and La Candeur still have some strength in reserve, however, because, instead of going up to their dormitories at the hour required by the regulations, they have stayed up chatting in a deserted corner of the canteen, where good tips slipped into the hand of the *feldwebel* and a considerable remuneration accorded to Mother Klupfel, assure them an almost absolute security for a few hours.

The Klupfel canteen never closes, by day or night, since the war began, because of the uninterrupted movement of the workers departing for the workshops or coming back from them. Usually, it's necessary to see the urgency with which Fräulein Emma and Fräulein Ida serve Munich beer, "delicatessens" and KK bread[21] to the workers and the soldiers who come to sit at the long and dusty tables in the big hall.

---

[21] Instead of feeding prisoners of war real bread, which was in short supply, the Germans fed them "KK bread", from *Kleie und Kartoffeln* [bran and potatoes], whose recipe remains uncertain and was probably variable.

That big hall connects with several other small rooms reserved for NCOs, the Klupfel family or certain private suppers. One of them has been rented by the French prisoners working in the factory. It is in that one that we find Rouletabille and his companion sitting in front of the remains of a supper that is still making La Candeur grimace.

Rouletabille has left the connecting door ajar, and from where he is sitting he can see everything that happens in the big hall. That gradually empties; the clients are complaining about the sudden disappearance of Fräulein Emma and Fräulein Ida. Mother Klupfel, who can no longer stay upright on her weary old legs has told them that her daughters, worn out, have gone upstairs to bed, but the obstinately closed door of a certain private room and the presence of two firemen's coats and red caps hanging on two hooks near that door is sufficient to certain imaginations overheated by the Munich.

Fräulein Emma and Fräulein Ida, if certain belated clients can be believed, are in the process of taking super with the owners of the aforementioned firemen's coats and red caps. Someone has even added that if the fiancés of those demoiselles, who are presently working in the foundry, were to have any suspicion of what is going on, they would not conceive any satisfaction from the awareness—to which one regular, who appears to be up to date with such matters, replies that Messieurs the fiancés would not care, being desirous that the two young ladies should amass an honorable dowry.

That final reflection seems to win the agreement of everyone. The last clients go to the door that opens on to the courtyard of the *arbeiterheim*.

Rouletabille did not let any of these movements escape him. In the meantime, La Candeur was muttering into his sleeve: "And to think that I still don't know what we came here to do! I don't know what you're planning, but there are three hundred thousand men here. What do you expect the two of us to do against three hundred thousand?"

"There aren't only two of us," said Rouletabille, abruptly. "There are three."

"Three! Where's the third, then?"

After darting a glance into the next room, Rouletabille leaned toward La Candeur's ear and said: "Vladimir's here.'"

The other started. "No! Where is he, then?"

"In the city, at the Essener-Hoff."

"Damn! Is it really possible? And what is he doing at the Essener-Hoff?"

"Waiting for my orders."

"Well, he might have to wait for a long time!"

"They've already reached him."

La Candeur considered Rouletabille admiringly for a moment. "You've sent them to him by post?" he asked, not without a certain irony.

"Exactly."

"Oh! God—and has he replied?"

"And he's replied."

"That's better than playing pitch-and-toss. How do you do it?"

"Well, we take paper, a pen and ink, of course, like everyone else…plus a certain little grid that allows us to insert into a letter of utter banality the words that correspond more particularly to our personal preoccupations."

"I understand the grid, but what I don't understand is how you can correspond."

"It's quite simple, though. You know that for four days I've been able to do almost as I wish in Richter's private offices, and I haven't spent all my time drawing designs for sewing-machines. Nothing's been easier than for me to slip an envelope into the stack of the engineer's correspondence, before someone comes to fetch it at a fixed time, which is in no way different from the others, and bears the postmark of the *kommando*. It is, therefore, a sacred object that no one dares allow to go astray, and which is religiously delivered into the hands of Nelpas Pacha, the representative of Turkish interests in regard to the House of Krupp, presently resident in the Essener-Hoff."

"Who's Nelpas Pacha?"

"Idiot! It's Vladimir. It's a name that Princes Botosani found for him, as if by chance, before he left Paris to go in her delightful company to the enchanted shores of the Bosphorus!"

"And who's this Princess Botosani?"

"I'll tell you all that in a few years' time. It would take too long today. Follow the movement carefully: Vladimir replies to me by writing to Richter, with whom he's entered into a business relationship, to the orders that I sent him in my first letter. I go through Richter's post at my leisure. Vladimir's envelope has a little mark; I open it, if it's not already open, and I confiscate the letter or let it remain—it doesn't matter. Anyone can read our prose; there's nothing in it but matters relating to sewing-machines. It's necessary to have the grid to discover another meaning."

"It is, indeed, quite simple," La Candeur concluded, ecstatically, "but only you can think of such things. Tell me, though, does Vladimir tell you interesting things in his letters?"

"You can believe it! I hear from him everything's that's happening in Essen, and he hears from me everything that's happening in the factory, or nearly."

"Yes, there must be a lot of gossip in Richter's house."

"All the more so as no one suspects that I'm always there to listen in...and Richter trusts me. I'll tell you something that will certainly cheer you up: I've just signed a partnership contract with him, for a magnificent project. I'm going to make a lot of money, La Candeur! I'm going to be rich!"

"What? You're going into partnership with the Boche now?"

"To begin with, Richter isn't Boche—he's Swiss, from Zurich. We're already good friends. He was so pleased with the first plans I gave him that he's invited me to his engagement party, so there!"

"Impossible!"

"Pooh! He could do no less for his partner. And do you know where he's holding his engagement party?"

"At the factory—in General von Berg's house?"

"Not at all! At the Essener-Hoff, my dear chap."

"And you've accepted?"

"Gladly. It will certainly give me an opportunity to chat at greater length with our friend Vladimir."

"Good! You have all the luck! And when shall I get to see him—Vladimir?"

Roulctabille suddenly stood up, and went to the door to the big hall, taking care to walk on tiptoe, and whispered to La Candeur: "Right away! You're going to see him right away!"

"What! In the factory?"

"In the factory."

"And who'll take us there?"

"If I told you," Rouletabille replied, "You wouldn't believe me. Now, shh!"

Nothing could be heard any longer but the snoring of Mother Klupfel, collapsed on the corner of a table. Rouletabille went into the big hall, headed for the hooks on which the two firemen's coats and red caps were hanging, took possession of those precious garments, returned with them to the room where La Candeur was waiting, and threw them on a table.

"Get dressed!"

And he did so himself. The uniform seemed to be made for him, and the little red helmet suited him delightfully. Unfortunately, La Candeur's frame accommodated the new garment rather poorly.

"You need to dispense the sleeves," the reporter whispered to him, and tilt the helmet to one side, so it looks chic."

A minute later, they were in the courtyard. Mother Klupfel was still snoring.

"Where are we going?" asked La Candeur.

"Anywhere the service demands," replied Rouletabille—and, pushing the little service cart used by firemen on patrol in the factory, which seemed to be waiting for them at the exit from the canteen, they had no difficulty walking past the guard post at the entrance to the courtyard of the *arbeiterheim* reserved for foreign workers and French prisoners.

The little cart had a compartment in which everything was contained necessary to stop or limit the initial progress of a fire: picks, spades axes, and, in a separate box, extinguishing gas-grenades. Finally, above the compartment, there was a light double ladder, which could be extended mechanically by hand.

"Old man," Rouletabille declared to his companion, as soon as they were in the heart of the factory, "I confess that I've had my eye on this ladder, and these coats and caps, since the night before last."

"To go see Vladimir?" suggested La Candeur, who, in the bewilderment into which all these precipitate and incomprehensible events had plunged him, now only had one thought in his mind: seeing Vladimir.

"Of course! To go see Vladimir, and a few other people that one would have great difficulty getting to if one didn't have a ladder and a fireman's coat and cap."

"There's no doubt about it—you think of everything."

They had just emerged from the dark shadow of the high walls of the *arbeiterheim*, however, and came to a sudden halt before an unexpected spectacle.

"It's beautiful, Hell!" sighed La Candeur.

They had never been in the factory by night; they had only ever heard its terrible din, which never died away, any more than the fire of its crucibles, but it was necessary for their eyes to be removed from the darkness to embrace at a stroke the horrible splendor of that chaos in flames. The slightest crack in a doorway open to the interior labor suddenly lit up the night with a fulgurant glow; the red plumes of tall chimneys writhed above their heads in the midst of whirlwinds of noxious smoke, blacker than the sky. Other fulgurances battered by the wind descended and dispersed in an eternal rain of fire and hot ash.

"Let's go!" whispered Rouletabille. "Courage, Le Candeur!"

And La Candeur, consternated but docile, condemned to turn in the accursed furnace without knowing what crime had sent him down to that Gehenna, repeated: "Let's go—since we have to."

One reference-point seemed to guide Rouletabille through that night of flame: the high walls of the octagonal tower whose steps he had climbed with Richter—the water tower. They arrived there without any inconvenience. They went through the midst of all the shadows that inhabited the roads bordered by roaring forges without anyone asking them a question.

At the water tower, Rouletabille paused briefly, waited until the vicinity was deserted, and then, still pushing his handcart, slipped between two enormous buildings whose walls, devoid of doors, had a kind of river of darkness between them. The young men were immediately swallowed up by that protective darkness, and soon fund themselves facing an edifice that had been deliberately isolated, as much as possible, from the great cacophony of labor. It was the house in which the director of the Energy Laboratory, Hans, lived with his daughter Helena and his prisoner Nicole.

Rouletabille knew that Nicole's window was the last in the left-hand corner, on the first floor. He also knew that Nicole was never alone at night—that a woman watched her incessantly—and that there were bars on Nicole's window. What, then, was he hoping to do? Why had he suddenly approached that wall? Why did he boldly and rapidly deploy the entire length of his ladder and support it on the roof, as if his duty as a fire-fighter demanded that he go to check that the building's superstructure was not in any danger in consequence of some falling flaming debris that he had observed? Why—because he wanted to see Nicole, whom he had not seen since the terrible scene when she had put into his hands the right to kill her.

No, Nicole had not come back again to Richter's design-studio with Helena, and the reporter had waited in vain for an opportunity to communicate with her.

As Rouletabille was about to set foot on the ladder, La Candeur said to him: "If someone comes, what should I do?"

"Nothing. You're doing your duty and I'm doing mine."

"If it's an officer, who speaks to me, I won't be able to reply."

"So don't reply."

"And if he persists?"

"Knock him out."

And Rouletabille climbed his ladder, going past a window permanently illuminated by a muted night-light—and as he went past he looked in. On her bed, directly opposite, against the back wall, he saw Nicole lying down, supporting her head in one hand, her eyes wide open.

Insomnia was afflicting the unfortunate young woman. She seemed lost in a profound dream, perhaps more cruel than those which pursued her in her sleep.

She looked up, however, and must have perceived Rouletabille's shadow at the window, because she got up quietly and snuffed out the night-light set on her bedside table.

The reporter no longer knew what to think or do. He had not forgotten that they still had to fear the female guard, doubtless asleep for the moment, but who might suddenly wake up and raise the alarm. On the other hand, it seemed to him that he could hear the murmur of voices on the other side of the wall, and he feared being taken by surprise, immobile on his ladder.

He climbed a few more rungs, his eyes still fixed on the window. Then, at the window, pressed against the glass, the pained and anguished face of Nicole appeared, fantastically illuminated by the intermittent gleams rending the ink-black sky.

Rouletabille made a sign to the young woman, and went back down the rungs he had just mounted. Almost immediately, the window was cautiously opened by a crack, and Nicole leaned out into the mystery of the night.

Rouletabille whispered to her: "I don't see you any more—why? It's absolutely necessary that you accept the invitation that Fräulein Hans will give you to her engagement party."

The reporter waited for a reply, but something new must have happened in the room, for the window snapped shut and the pale apparition disappeared.

Now the darkness was profound, and the murmur of voices on the other side of the wall was renewed. A few words reached Rouletabille and excited his curiosity. He went up on to the roof, slid along the gutter and, having arrived at its extremity, leaned over. On the threshold of Hans's dwelling, a light coming room inside showed him two men, who were chatting while smoking their pipes.

He recognized that taller and more powerfully-built of the two by his butler's uniform: it was the guard who always accompanied Nicole on her excursions with Helena. The other had to be the concierge.

Rouletabille clearly heard fragmentary sentences. "Since Wednesday, I've been able to go back to sleep at my own place…it's still the same…except tomorrow, the service will start to be hard again…yes, they're going out…going for a ride…seems that it's necessary to be seen…after Wednesday, I was pretty sure that I'd be rid of it all..."

The other replied: "Yes. We all thought here that it was finished."

"Oh well—and over there, Princess Botosani said: 'she'll be dead tomorrow.'"

"And now, she's much better! It's incredible how resilient these young women are—not to mention that, when they want her to look well, they can feed her an uncommon elixir..."

"Give me a pinch of tobacco, my old Franz, so that I can smoke one last pipe before going back to the house..."

Rouletabille did not hear any more. Now he knew the perfectly simple reason why he had not seen Nicole again. Fulbert's daughter had been very ill after the scene of the interview with Serge Kaniewsky—so ill that they had had to take her to a hospital immediately, or at least to a house of rest—where Princess Botosani, presently at the Essener-Hoff with Vladimir, had doubtless had the opportunity to give her some care…for, by virtue of her well-known cosmopolitanism, that charming woman must have had the pleasure of donning a nurse's uniform in Germany, as in Paris. Now, Nicole was much better, and there was nothing astonishing about that, her weakness being primarily the result of a mental state that could be transformed from one day to the next.

Quite content with what he had just learned, the reporter went back to his ladder, climbed down again, observing that there was no further apparition of Nicole at the window and that the nigh-light in the room had not been lit again. Then he let himself slide down the ladder and fell into La Candeur's arms.

The latter said: "I can't do this any longer. Twice, now a big devil of a fireman-sergeant has gone past, looking at me oddly. The second time, he spoke to me! You can imagine that I was in a panic. I didn't know what he said to me, but at hazard, I answered '*Ja!*' leaning over my cart as if I were very busy. It seems that that did the trick, since he continued on his way, throwing a '*Gute nacht!*' at me, to which I didn't even reply because of the accent. I don't trust myself, you know—there's only *Ja* that I know in German and can pronounce properly. The rest of the language, it's better not to speak. Now, let's get away!"

"Yes," said Rouletabille. "*En route*. We don't have anything more to do here."

They restored the ladder to its customary height and departed promptly, pushing their little cart.

Once again it was necessary for them to go along avenues that were cluttered and very busy. They threw themselves into it bravely, almost running, as if they had received orders to go to a place where their services were required as soon as possible.

Suddenly, they saw a big man in a red cap loom up in front of them: the foreman-sergeant that La Candeur had mentioned.

"It's him!" sighed La Candeur! "Him again! He'll see us!"

Rouletabille slowed his pace and passed bravely under the nose of the terrible NCO. The latter, addressing La Candeur, said in a harsh voice, in the jargon of a Boche soldier: "I've already told you to put your cap on straight! Make sure I don't have to tell you again. If you were in my section, you'd get to know me, you stubborn swine!"

"Pay no attention," grunted Rouletabille. "My comrade's a bit deaf—I'll talk to him." And he hastened his steps, taking an obscure side-street to the left—but the other followed them.

"What does the animal want now?" groaned La Candeur., wiping large droplets of sweat from his forehead. "He scares me, that one! He won't let up, you know!"

"Straighten your cap!" said Rouletabille, rapidly. "He wants you to be properly dressed."

"Damn it! I can't get my arms into the sleeves!"

"Don't stop! Don't stop—but pretend to be putting them on…perhaps he'll let us go."

La Candeur straightened his cap and tried to put his arm in a sleeve while continuing to march.

"Oh, I can't, I can't! They're sleeves for a doll!"

"Sure! You'd rather have his coat!"

"It'd fit me like a glove," La Candeur agreed, beginning to tremble.

"Not to mention that it would promote you to sergeant on the spot—which isn't disagreeable."

"Don't joke, Rouletabille. Here he comes! Here he comes! He'll have us, I tell you. I'm scared!"

"Keep going, without paying any attention, and keep your coat on your shoulders. If you're as scared at all that, so much the better."

"Why's that?"

"Because when he gets close to us, you're going to turn round calmly and give him your 'fearful punch.'"

"Like the Turk in the Black Castle?"

"Like the Turk. He mustn't make a sound. If you mess it up, I wouldn't give a pfennig for both our skins!"

"One will never be tranquil again in this vale of tears!" groaned La Candeur, literally quivering with fear—but Rouletabille saw with pleasure that his arm was free and that he was already swinging it, while clenching a most imposing fist.

At that moment, the *feldwebel* caught up with them, cursing and gesticulating.

It happened as planned. La Candeur turned round "calmly," as Rouletabille had recommended, raised his right arm as if to salute, and suddenly brought his "fearful punch" down on the NCOs head.

The other did not even utter a sigh. He fell as if thunderstruck, into a gutter along the wall, through which black water was running.

"Damn it! He's going to get my lovely coat dirty!" La Candeur exclaimed, falling upon the body and ripping it off him. Then he turned to Rouletabille.

"Can you believe that I've killed him?" he asked.

"Like a pole-axed ox," the reporter replied. "I warned him. But this is no time for making speeches! Give me your coat and cap, so I can put them in the cart, and put on his uniform. Put on his cap! There you are—lovely as a star! And I have to obey your orders! Everyone will leave us in peace, now that you've been promoted."

"What are we going to do with the body?" asked La Candeur. "We can't leave him here."

"No—put him over your shoulder, quickly."

"We've got a pick and a shovel—perhaps we could bury him?" La Candeur suggested, hoisting the corpse on to his back with Rouletabille's help.

"Do you think so? Perhaps we should also build him a monument with a cross on top? Let's go—march!"

A few paces away, Rouletabille had already see that the stream ran into a large pond that must be very deep, to judge by the quantity of dirty and steaming water that was emerging from the cast-iron pipes and pouring into it; the enormous opening of a drain collected the unclean water in order to carry it God only knew where…but the bottom of the basin must never run dry, and the reporter had immediately concluded that it would be an admirable tomb for a Boche NCO who had to disappear without leaving any trace.

It was with difficulty that Rouletabille detached one of the two knotted ropes that were in their cart, but the rope was necessary to attach two large stones that were protecting the entrance to a garage to the *feldwebel*'s neck and feet.

After tying the NOC up, they dropped him into the little infernal lake, and did not stick around to contemplate the ripples that the fall of the weighted body made in the bubbling water.

A few minutes later, they found themselves back in the midst of the nocturnal blaze of the prodigious forge.

"Where are we going now?! La Candeur demanded, anxiously, thinking that they had had enough adventures for one night. "Are we going back soon? If we don't get back in time, the two firemen will come out of Mother Klupfel's howling that someone's stolen their kit."

"Do you think so? They'll think it's a joke— especially when they can't find their little cart."

"You aren't going to give it back?"

"What do you expect me to do with it? I can't keep it in my pocket."

"So?"

"So, when we've finished making use of it, we'll find it in some corner where they'll be able to find it. Except that I'd better warn you immediately that they'll search in vain for the two ropes, the rope-ladder, the pick, the spade and the two axes."

"And you don't think they'll squeal?"

"No—because of the missing coats and caps, they won't say a word. They're at fault, old chap—and I tell you that they'll think that their comrades, jealous of their success with Fräulein Ida and Fräulein Emma, have played a joke on them. Have no fear—they'll get out of it as best they can…but they won't complain. Anyway, they can do as they wish, for it isn't me who'll give them back their coats and caps!"

"Perhaps you're wrong! What are you going to do with them?"

"They're so convenient for taking a walk."

"Well, I'll just say one thing, which is that I'm beginning to think, perfectly, that I've had enough of going for walks. Suppose we went back to bed! Don't you agree?"

"Certainly not. We're doing very nicely here. One comes, one goes, one can wander anywhere one wants. One can see everything! One can learn! Just look! Don't you think this is wonderful: the spectacle of the foundry by night? You said it yourself: it's beautiful, Hell.

"I'm afraid that it might burn us."

But Rouletabille, without paying any further attention to his companion's bad mood, had suddenly accelerated his pace in such a way that La Candeur, who was then pushing the little cart, had difficulty keeping up with him.

"Where are you running off to like that?" he complained, from behind. "Are you sure you're not going crazy? Can't you see that there's a crowd up ahead? What are all these people doing? It's full of officers, old man! Don't go that way, damn it! Oh my God! But I'm not dreaming…Rouletabille! Rouletabille! Look, there, in that group behind the officers—it's Vladimir!"

"Well, didn't I promise you that you'd see him to-night?" Rouletabille whispered to him, stopping suddenly. "Now veer to the left. Look over there, between the big crane and the locomotive. See that man standing at the entrance to the workshop—don't you recognize him? Don't you recognize him? He's well illuminated by the flames emerging from the crucibles, though. One might think that he were in the fire. Yes! The man raising his arm, who looks as if he's commanding the fire!"

"But that's...that the Emperor!" murmured La Candeur, recoiling instinctively. Terrified, he immediately added: "Let's get out of here!"

"On the contrary," said Rouletabille. "Let's follow him."

Chapter XVI
The Master of Fire

It was while shivering that Dante arrived at the final threshold of the Inferno, and perceived the monarch of the Empire of Tears. It was with chattering teeth that Rouletabille's companion rested his fearful gaze on the God of Fire, the modern Lucifer. Tottering, La Candeur leaned on his audacious friend's shoulder, not so much in order to follow him as to try to stop him.

Yes, the man they had before them was the very man who called himself the Terror of the World. His face, like that of Satan, was red with fire. An insane pride elevated his stature and inflated his armor. His flamboyant helmet, with bore a bird of prey, crowned him with a frightful crest. His hideous features assembled in his face all the fatal marks that have stigmatized the fallen archangels since the Creature turned against his Creator.

And where, then, could the rage and vengeance, after the devastated dream, be expressed in sharper relief on the face of the accursed one, than in the cycle in which destruction prepared its weapons and its thunderbolts: at Krupp's!—between the rivers of flame that only consented to cool down in order to reignite more fiercely over the world reduced to ashes! Do not seek elsewhere for the abode of evil; it is there; there is the heart of crimes and torments; it is there that it necessary to see the man!

Tonight, he has gathered around him illustrious friends, timid allies and important neutral individuals

150

who have not dared to refuse his invitation; he has made that cohort come a long way to visit his inferno. He needs to be seen in all his force and malediction. Some emerging therefrom will be reaffirmed in their faith; others will resume their route, terrorized. Where, better than at Essen, can terror be forged?

"Let's get out of here!" begged La Candeur. "I don't want to look at him anymore! He's too ugly!"

"No, that man isn't ugly. A monster isn't ugly. A monster is a monster—which is to say, something outside humanity and universal life, who can't be compared to anything else."

The man is incomparable. There is no rival to Satan in Gehenna, because he is the only being entirely at home there. He is the soul of disaster and ruination, and it is his breath that passes over the furnaces of Essen and gives life to the molten steel, and the form required in order that Death might be more powerful upon the earth, and might laugh at all the obstacles imagined by the fear or prudence of human beings.

Where, then, is that primordial era in which Skeletal Death came to humans with a scythe in his hand? Now, he scythes with a 420.

Fire can refuse nothing to its master. Fire gives him everything he desires, and, at this very moment, like a chained dragon that accepts its slavery, fire is licking the master with all its tongues.

Before the open crucibles, and amid the tumultuous delight of the giant hammers, the Master of Fire explains the infernal miracle over which he presides; from the depths of the furnaces, through roaring mouths, slaves withdraw blocks of flame that they deposit in a matrix. Then a powerful arm advances, moved by an invincible and docile force, toward the matrix obstructed by the red ingot. Then the arm sinks into the soft and incandescent material, which molds itself around it. When the arm has pierced the block of steel from end to end, it is placed in another, narrower matrix, and another, stouter, arm reiterates the work of the first. Then the ingot becomes a tube, whole walls are thinned by each new thread. When it is finished, one has a canon. It only remains to score it. It is rapid. It is the new procedure with which, in two hours, one can make a cannon. Once, when the boring was cold, it took a day and a half! And Death was waiting! Death, the peevish spouse of the Master of the House, must not be made to wait...

For two hours, the Master has been showing his guests around his domain in this fashion. All the workshops, all the gulfs, open before him and his retinue. Even the most secret forges, which no profane eye has yet dared to penetrate, open momentarily in order that the man's pride might be satisfied, and the publicity of terror that he has decided to spread throughout the world perfected.

There are journalists in that troop running at the monster's heels. Rouletabille recognizes colleagues from beyond the Rhine, with whom he has associated professionally in Paris, when they were peacetime correspondents there—and, in many ways, the preparers of war. The reporter is glad that the fulgurant presence of the Master dazzles all their eyes and leaves him in shadow.

In the shadows, with his companion, he follows the escort. He makes himself part of it. Both of them seem to be there by order, with the bodyguards and the military flunkeys whom the steps of the Emperor of Fire always drag behind him.

If anyone interrogates Rouletabille, he has a ready response that will formulate the order received to accompany the sovereign of Essen everywhere, just in case fire should forget its servitude. Two firemen, armed with extinguishers, are a safety measure, even for the Devil, if he disguises himself in human flesh in order to come to the earth.

No one pay any attention to firemen—who, themselves, pay attention to everything.

And now they find themselves in front of the Energy Laboratory.

The troop goes into the central building, over the threshold on which Chief Engineer Hans greets his Master.

They go through rooms where work is presently going on that would not have put the pride and audacity of the alchemists to shame. Will not radium permit the realization, in the near future, of all the dreams of the occult science of the Middle Ages? That is what the man who knows everything explains.

While other peoples still linger over work on the recent discovery of the dematerialization of matter, here they are working on its rematerialization. Instead of following the sequence of successive transformations of radiant matter, which always operate by successive degradations of energy, the people working here are in the business of physiological reconstruction: taking the elementary particles of the ultimate substances of which our material world is constructed, and reconstructing the edifice of the world at will! A world that will no longer obey the ordinary laws of physics! Remaking the world! Behold the dream of the monster who has put God's good work in his pocket!

Listen to the damned:

"If it is already certain that, by taking individual atoms one by one and manipulating them with magical fingers, one can imagine selecting them adroitly enough to remake, with the energy of decay, energy useful for any purpose, there is every reason to think that, by choosing among the materials that enter into the structure of the atom, we should be able to engage them in new combinations that will permit the renewal of useful energy. Where has this work got to, at the present moment? Excellencies, Messieurs, it is not my privilege, as yet, to tell you, but while we await the time when we shall be able to recreate the world"—the Antichrist declares with a hideous smile—"we shall continue to show you the means we have made to destroy it! Yes, the reason I have gathered you here, is in order that you will be able to tell the world that we have its fate in our hand, and that our hand has only to make a sign, for the richest cities in the world, with their inhabitants and their civilization, to disappear in a matter of minutes! And that without our having to leave here!"

At this formidable statement, a visible frisson ran through the crowd—but the Emperor had made a sign, and Hans had opened a door opening into a corridor. Everyone trooped into it behind him.

They arrived by this route in a rather large laboratory—the very same one in which Malet had worked. That laboratory had been separated into several sections, forming veritable private rooms in each corner, closed either by curtains or by doors.

One of these small laboratories had a glazed door, the windows of which were illuminated by a vivid red glare.

When everyone had assembled in the central room, the Emperor said, in a low voice, pointing to the glazed door: "Go and look through that window, and you will see a man working on an admirable project: a universal remedy by means of radium. You must have heard mention of that man. He is a genius; his name is Théodore Fulbert. He's a Frenchman. He is our prisoner. I did not want the hazards of war to interrupt the course of work destined to cure all the ills of humankind—if humankind consents to be cured!—and we have put our laboratory at his disposal. You see that we are not total barbarians!"

Having said that, he went to the door himself, and leaned toward the window; then he turned round and made a sign indicating that the others should come closer.

The forward movement had already commenced when it came to an abrupt halt. A few guests even recoiled.

That was because a strange and fantastic face had just appeared at the pane: eyes of fire; a grimacing mouth; a vast, tormented forehead hollowed out by profound wrinkles; framed by hair whose white wisps were entangled, twisting as if on the head of a gorgon...and that entire physiognomy, which seemed to be quivering in somber fury, was flamboyant in the red light of the laboratory, seemingly as sublime as genius and as terrible as madness.

The Emperor himself, at that apparition, had taken a step backwards. The grim face had turned toward him and was burning him with its frightful gaze.

Then the Emperor, as if to make fun of the instinctive movement that had caused him to recoil, said in a loud voice: "Théodore Fulbert definitely does not want to be disturbed while he is working!"

Immediately, insensate cried erupted behind the window:

"Murderer! Murderer! Murderer!"

Chapter XVII
The Greater Blackmail of the World

Singularly enough, before this clamor, the monarch of Essen was untroubled, and manifested no anger.

With an imperious finger, he pointed at the door behind which Fulbert continued to rage and howl, and Hans opened it. Immediately, Fulbert rushed out, and then stopped abruptly on his shaking legs. Thus a wild beast bounds out of its cage to enter the circus arena, and suddenly suspends its surge before the innumerable and unexpected faces of the spectators.

Fulbert gazed, as if bewildered, at the officers, the diplomats, the engineers and the journalists: the entire gaudily-clad troop surrounding the tamer; doubtless he was wondering, in his confused thoughts, for what obscure reason he had suddenly been produced, at liberty, before such an exceptional escort.

But a furious lion cannot reflect for long, and Fulbert, shaking his white mane, resumed roaring: "Murderer! Murderer! Murderer!"

Guards were already running forward, but the Emperor immobilized them with a terrible gesture. "Let that man speak!" he said.

And "that man" spoke. He said:

"Behold the murderer of the world! Take care! If you do not kill the monster, the monster will kill you! And above all, take every precaution! Don't let yourselves be captured, like me—as he has captured my daughter, as he had captured my son-in-law! His Majesty has a long arm and a cunning hand! You might believe, in truth, that you are in a corner hidden from other men, but that is exactly where he will seek you out, and will bring you here, bund hand and foot, into his forge, and he will make you work for him, night and day, like it or not! And if you refuse, he will invent tortures that you will be unable to resist!

"Take care! Take care! If you have a daughter, he will torture your daughter. And if you have the accursed courage to let your daughter die, before your eyes, without surrendering your secret, he will bring your daughter's fiancé down to the cell where the poor girl is dying—and then the fiancé will talk, and work for that man! And the world may tremble, for the secret will have been surrendered—the secret that ought to kill war, because when one possesses such a secret, war will no longer be possible!

"Yes, it's me; it's me, Théodore Fulbert—you have heard mention, have you not, of Théodore Fulbert, an innocent scientist who was a friend to all humankind?— it's me who discovered a machine…a mighty machine... Well, the monster has stolen it from me! I have killed war, but to the profit of the monster! If you do not kill him, tremble! For I tell you this, I tell you this: he will kill you or reduce you to servitude. How can he still exist? He will devour you! I tell you that he will devour you! Tear his heart out, then, and throw it to the dogs! Murderer! Murderer! Murderer!"

Had the Emperor smiled? Shrugged his shoulders? Sniggered? It only required one tiny gesture on the part of the detested adversary suddenly to multiply tenfold the rage of an animal whose blood was already boiling. At any rate, Fulbert, losing all semblance of humanity, suddenly hurled himself at the Emperor with the furious bound of a slavering beast, with blood on his teeth and fingernails clawed.

This time, there was only just time to intervene, and two guards were not too many to hold the enraged old man back, throw him back into his workroom and lock the door behind him.

"That man is mad!" proclaimed all those who were accompanying the Emperor.

The Emperor, however, said: "No, he isn't mad. He's not mad, but simply furious at the fine trick that I've played on him, and which I shall explain to you."

With these words, still enigmatic to many, he drew his entire retinue into the room that they had initially entered, where they were shielded from Fulbert's shouts, moans and curses.

There, having lit a cigarette, and smiling, he began:

"Gentlemen, Fulbert is so far from mad that it is no idle boast when he says that he has found a device such that no war is possible against the man who possesses it. When I took possession of Fulbert and those who were working with them—which is to say, his daughter and his daughter's fiancé—Fulbert, as he has just told you, in the language of a prophet of doom, inspired by the basest hatred, was on the point of unleashing against me and against Germany the cruelest thunderbolt that a human brain has ever been able to conceive. That thunderbolt, I have stolen from him! And it is me that it shall serve. Is that not good strategy?"

Immediately, those assembled there were no longer able to find words enough to express their admiration, but the Emperor reestablished silence with a gesture and continued:

"The machine! It is me who has it, and I will show it to you—and you will understand Fulbert's fury...and my calm, and my forgiveness. For I forgive that man, who wanted to destroy my country, but who has finally furnished the means for German *Kultur* to spread its benefits over the entire world. As Fulbert desired, gentlemen, his machine will be a machine of peace, but peace dictated by Germany, for the greater good of humankind!

"One more word, gentlemen, before we continue on our way. Fulbert is not mad, but he is a liar! To obtain his secret, we have not tortured anyone! His daughter, who has never been in very good health, is as well as can be expected today, and is treated as a friend by engineer Hans' own daughter, General von Berg's niece. At the same time as you will be shown the infernal machine that will make us the masters of the world, you will be introduced to the man who surrendered Fulbert's secret. It is his assistant, the Pole Serge Kaniewsky, the anarchist who was condemned by a French court to give years in prison merely for having held forbidden opinions. You will understand that France is not dear to Kaniewsky's heart, and that it did not require any effort on our part to convince him, in return for a small fortune, to assist us in destroying Paris!"

"Destroying Paris!" tremulous voices were heard to say. "Your Majesty is going to destroy Paris!"

"I shall destroy everyone who resists me! Come, gentlemen."

While the Emperor was speaking thus, Fulbert, at the other end of the laboratory, collapsed on to the floor of the vast furnace of his laboratory, with his head in his hands, weeping. Yes, now he was crying like a baby! And his sobs, after the insensate fury that had shaken his aged carcass, were a benefit. They saved him, by soothing him. He found therein an unaccustomed gentleness, and bathed in his tears as in a refreshing wave.

He was drawn out of that dolorous torpor by the sound of a small stone falling nearby. It was a stone that had fallen down the chimney—and it certainly had not fallen of its own accord, for it was wrapped in a piece of paper, of which the inventor surreptitiously took possession, and unfolded with a tremulous hand, having made sure that he was quite alone and that no one would catch him.

The unfortunate scientist read: *Hope! You have not been abandoned. Be at work here every night, at four o'clock in the morning, and do exactly what you are instructed by one who signs himself: TITANIA.*

The procession was now retracing its steps through the entire factory. La Candeur, who had just been rejoined by Rouletabille, no longer took his eyes off a certain person who was gradually drawing closer to our two firemen. That was Nelpas Pacha, who must have been slightly fatigued by all the infernal tribulations, because he was visibly limping. For a moment, he allowed all his colleagues and the officers accompanying him to draw ahead of him, stopping as if he were paying particular attention to some task, which actually had nothing special about it—and then he resumed his progress. To catch up with his group, however, he had to go past Rouletabille, and he had the time to hear a few words clearly pronounced although in a low voice: "Everything's going well. It's essential that you attend the engagement party for von Berg's niece."

Nelpas Pacha nodded his head in a fashion that could not be misunderstood. He could not have furnished any more categorical response if he had pronounced the word: "Understood!" And he accelerated his pace.

"He didn't even look to me!" sighed La Candeur.

"But you looked at him too much, you great imbecile!"

"Thanks for the telling off!"

"Shut up!"

The two companions did not say another word until they reached the entrance to the famous wooden wall that enclosed the space reserved for the construction of what had been believed until now to be a new model of Zeppelin.

Once there, Rouletabille could not suppress a gesture of satisfaction. "Good!" he murmured, between his teeth. "We're going in through gate B..."

The Emperor and his entourage had already passed over the redoubtable threshold. The two foremen, extinguishers in their belts, passed through in their turn.

Immediately to the left there was a wooden building which served as a porter's lodge as well as a military post and emergency station, as there was at all the gates. The door of that small house was open, and they could see a large common room in which, after the procession had passed through, soldiers resumed their places on the benches or sat around the tables, relighting their pipes.

A fireman, recognizable by his coat and red cap, was leaning over a desk set against the wall, writing some kind of report. A mirror was hanging in front of the desk, attached to the wall. Slightly to the left of the table there was a small window, with a single pane, which looked outside and must permit the concierge, before opening the door, to examine from within the people who wanted to go into the enclosure outside the times when the workers went in and out.

It was also in that small room that the distribution was made of the identity tags that were received there when the shifts changed.

With a keen-eyed glance, Rouletabille took account of the distribution of the room and the places occupied by the people in it. He said to La Candeur: "Follow me, and whatever happens, play dumb and don't get upset."

When they went into the room, the soldiers who had started smoking and chatting did not pay any attention to them. Only the fireman, who had finished his report and had turned round, looked at them curiously.

The redoubtable appearance of La Candeur imposed itself upon him immediately, but, as Rouletabille headed for the desk that he had just quit, the fireman could not resist the temptation to say to him: "What are you doing here? Your section has no business here."

Rouletabille indicated the terrifying La Candeur with a sideways glance, and pronounced the simple word: "*Polizei!*"

Immediately, the other, who had just seen the Emperor and his cortege pass by, jumped to the conclusion that he was confronted by important members of the secret police, and rectified his stance.

"Not a word!" Rouletabille whispered to him. "Let me make my report."

The fireman saluted and Rouletabille started writing on the sheets of blank paper that were on the desk.

Strangely enough, although his handwriting was usually cramped and untidy, he was careful on this occasion to form the letters very neatly, and was undoubtedly in fear of blots, for he had only traced a few words when he carefully dried them with the blotting-pad with which the desk was equipped.

He remained there for ten minutes, during which La Candeur's brows became increasingly furrowed, because he was increasingly nervous—after which the reporter calmly folded up the piece of paper and put it into his pocket. Then, with the satisfied expression of a man who has finished a chore, he went back to La Candeur and said: "Let's go."

"Are we finished?" implored La Candeur, as soon as they were out of the guard-post.

"Bah! We've only just begun, old man!"

"Damn!"

"Now we have to trot to catch up with the procession. But first, hang on a moment!"

They were presently isolated in a shadowy corner invaded by all kinds of detritus that had been swept there. Rouletabille meticulously tore up the pieces of paper he had just covered with magnificent writing and threw them on to a heap of ashes.

"Right!" said La Candeur. "It was well worth the trouble of making me spend the worst minutes of my life waiting for you! You've never taken so long to write an article! And now you've thrown it on the rubbish heap!"

Rouletabille close his mouth and showed him the procession, which was coming back in their direction.

They rejoined it as it penetrated into the monstrous building whose fantastic silhouette dominated the factory and the city, and which was the subject of all conversations from Dusseldorf to Duisburg and the entire infernal plain between the Rhine and the Ruhle.

The first impression one had, on entering that prodigious vessel, was compounded from two elements: a sense of being overwhelmed and amazed by the truly colossal dimensions of the cradle, whose length was almost a kilometer and was capable of containing the most monstrous of leviathans within its titanic framework of wood and iron, along with its launch-tube, which broadened at its highest extremity into a vast "ladle." It was impossible, at first, to appreciate the height of the scaffolding, the walkways and the flying steel bridges, rolling on their castors, from one extremity to the other of that iron vaults, whose arch closed more than forty meters above the ground. It transported crews of workers who, at that distance, seemed to be the size of penholders. Yes, it was all overwhelming, and all amazing, by reason of the formidable tumult quivering along the hammered flanks of the *Titania*.

Overwhelmed, amazed and also dazzled by the sheets of electric light poured down by a thousand stars suspended from a wooden sky that would only open again to let the redoubtable aircraft escape, Rouletabille paused momentarily, his heart pounding, and his soul filed with such anguish that drops of sweat were beading his temples. With a nervous, almost unconscious, gesture, he grasped his companion's arm.

"Well," he said, "now you see it—the three hundred meter canon! You can see that it wasn't a dream."

It was not a dream; that cannon, which was a torpedo-launching tube, was four hundred meters long.

It was there, almost complete: the Titania born in Fulbert's inflamed brain. And yet, if Fulbert had been able to see it, he would have died of grief!

Its menacing nose-cone was not turned toward the city cursed by men, but it was ready to depart for Paris—devoted, by the Emperor of Fire, to death and destruction.

That terrible thought returned all of Rouletabille's presence of mind and composure. "Let's follow the Emperor," he whispered to La Candeur, who seemed to be utterly bewildered, crushed by the colossal vision. He dragged him along.

They were behind the procession once again, as if they were following orders, and they saw everything, slipping between girders as thick as cathedral pillars in order to see better, running over precariously-balanced planks, and, without attracting any attention whatsoever, creeping close enough to the imperial speaker to hear him offer his brief explanations, which had to be shouted in order to rise above the tumult.

Thus they made a tour of the place, and found themselves with the others inside the tube and inside the torpedo itself, a steel cylinder such as had never been seen before, and inside which they could already see the steel partitions destined to carry the small cylinders as a mother carries her young...

The Emperor explained everything, giving details of the principal divisions of the engine, pausing at the hydraulic jacks that opened and closed the loading bay by means of steel hawsers, inviting admiration of the unprecedented dimensions of the compressed-air accumulators for the initial launch of the torpedo—which, as soon as it emerged from the tube, would be propelled henceforth by its own means. Finally, he took care to give full significance to the orientation of the apparatus: north-east/south-west...toward Paris!

And he added:

"At Paris first—for the tube can be reloaded and contain other *Titanias*, if necessary. And we can direct the tube toward any point on the earth's surface, as necessary, for the tube, as you will observe, can pivot on an enormous circular platform: a platform that can still serve at the last minute, once the temporary buildings that surround us have been demolished, to make the direction mathematically precise or to modify it. For example, we could as easily send the *Titania* to fall on London. If we aren't doing that, it's because there are people among us who don't like London, while everyone loves Paris—and the entire world will weep for it!"

Thus spoke the Monarch of Tears.

And in order that he might be more clearly understood, a sudden order was issued to suspend the resounding labor. Thus, it was in a silence all the more impressive because it succeeded an infernal din, that the Emperor continued, while all the neutral and allied journalists took out their notepads and took down the sacred words:

"Excellencies, gentlemen, you have seen the work! It will be completed in two months. In two months, if Paris has not heeded our voice of amity and forgiveness, Paris will be no more. We are not barbarians. We shall make known our conditions of peace. We want it to be durable, and such that German *kultur* will no longer be endangered anywhere in the world.

"We did not want this war, but since it has been forced upon us, it is only just that we profit from it at least to demand the space necessary for the development of our genius on all the continents. The World must understand that, or the World will die!

"Go forth, and repeat our words. With all our heart, moved by so many present miseries and by the anticipation of future catastrophes, we want to be heard by our worst enemies: those who know the power of the weapon that has been intended for use against us and which we are turning against them.

"You can tell them that you have seen working, in total liberty, for the completion of the most terrible machine ever to emerge from the human mind, the man who, with Fulbert, drew up its initial plans, carried out the first trials of its effect in England, and who consents today to make it serve as his vengeance against a city and a people who have condemned him and cursed him, for the realization of our designs for the future and the happiness of humankind!"

As he pronounced these final words, the Emperor indicated, half-suspended in space, strangely attached to the end of a catwalk from which one could look down on all the works of the *Titania*, the tormented silhouette of a man whose head was in his hands and who was looking down at what was happening beneath him with the eyes of a madman. It was the Pole, Serge Kaniewsky, Nicole's fiancé.

Had he heard the Emperor's final words? Was he embarrassed by all the eyes turning toward him? At any rate, he stood up, and walked at a slow pace toward other points and other catwalks. At the corner of one of them he crossed the path of a fireman who seemed to be making a tour of inspection, and who took the time to say, rapidly, as he passed him by:

"The walks will resume; raise the lid of the desk next to the window of Gate B and look at the blotting-pad in the mirror."

Chapter XVIII
The Engagement Party

The celebration of Helena Hans' engagement was not merely to be the occasion of a small family fête.

Rouletabille had known for a long time, having lent an attentive ear to the private conversations of Helena and Richter, that the Emperor was determined that the gala feast in question, presided over by General von Berg, would figure as an important episode in the tragi-comedy of blackmail that he had determined to play on the world stage, with the *Titania* in the wings. It was a matter of showing off the inventor's daughter there, at liberty, treated as a friend by Hans' daughter, and putting a stop, at a stroke, the stories of torture that were beginning to run around in diplomatic circles, which had already found an echo in certain Dutch socialist newspapers.

It was in a similar spirit that Wilhelm had taken it into his head to exhibit to his cortege of journalists, during the famous nocturnal factory visit, a Fulbert occupied in scientific research. As for the inventor's clamoring regarding the ill-treatment to which Nicole had been subjected, the presence of the young woman at the gala meal ought to rob them of all significance—and on the other hand, they undoubtedly had more than enough decisive means to employ against Nicole's dearly-beloved father to fear that she would say anything in public that was not to everyone's taste.

Nicole, having been invited by Helena, had initially refused—of which Rouletabille had not been unaware, and which had determined him to let her know that it was necessary to accept.

If, in order to enter into communication with her, he had had to resort to a nocturnal enterprise that was not without danger, it was because Nicole had not shown herself for several days with Helena in Richter's home. The excursions had ceased, and that had intrigued the reporter all the more because he had discovered their importance and their significance.

Before arriving at Richter's residence, Helena, every time she had Nicole beside her in her automobile, had always taken the same route, which went along the great wooden wall of the enclosure reserved for the *Titania*, and past Gate B, slowing down in front of the porter's window.

Now, behind that little window, at the appointed hour, Serge Kaniewsky was standing, in order that he thus could be allowed to see his fiancée, and who would not consent to work unless proof of that sort was provided that the woman he loved was still being treated appropriately and maintained in good health.

We know that the Pole had gone so far as to demand meetings, but we also know what had happened during the first of them, which was not followed by any other. Finally, we have learned how Rouletabille took advantage of Serge's repeated station at the desk at Gate B to the necessary instructions to Serge, by means of a blotting-pad, for an enterprise whose results we shall soon see.

Rouletabille and La Candeur, having followed the Emperor's cortege step by step, had got back into their lodgings that same night much more easily than such audacious and tragic peregrinations might have given them reason to fear. The possession of two—indeed, three—foremen's uniforms permitted them to do many things, however, while assuring them of a certain security.

It is also necessary not to forget that they continued to have at their disposal very useful objects: picks, spades, axes, ropes and rope-ladders, of which they could make all necessary use on the following nights.

Now, Rouletabille could communicate as he wished with Fulbert, with Nicole and with Serge, and he had an ongoing correspondence with Vladimir.

Finally, to crown all these fine results, he was fortunate enough to be invited to the famous engagement party—and in order that no one should be mistaken, that stroke of luck was entirely natural. The higher authorities were glad to show von Berg's guests, at the same time as the inventor Fulbert's daughter, a French engineer—for the Boche had not hesitated to award the Frenchman Talmar the title of engineer—working in partnership with a Swiss engineer within the Krupp factory, and working without restraint, in accordance with a contract freely made.

Two days before the lunch at the Essener-Hoff, Rouletabille, who was drawing a diagram of a new lever in his little office, taking great care to establish the differences and measurements that distinguished the lever in question from an old lever that he had set on the table in front of him, saw Helena and Nicole getting out of the automobile..

Immediately, he hid in his cupboard and waited.

Richter and Helena left Nicole in the design-studio in order to go up to the first floor to visit Richter's aged mother, who was a chronic invalid.

Rouletabille decided to take advantage of the fortunate solitude in which Fulbert's daughter had been left—

the butler-guard had remained in the vestibule, as usual—emerged from his hiding-place and prudently went to put an eye to the keyhole.

He was initially astonished that Nicole, who must, however, have been as desirous as he was to renew their conversation, did not even turn to look at the study in which she knew that he was working on her behalf. She was standing indifferently in front of a drawing-board and seemed to be following the lines traced on the paper, as if she had nothing else to do but kill time.

Rouletabille thought that such an attitude must have been dictated to her by prudence, and he waited—but he waited in vain for the head, which he could only see in profile, to turn in his direction. Finally, no longer being able to contain himself, he opened the door. This time, Nicole turned toward him, and even started, as if genuinely surprised to find that there was someone in the office.

"Oh, Monsieur you frightened me!" she said.

At the same moment, Richter's voice became audible in the corridor. "Yes, Mama is better. I think that she'll be able to attend the party."

Immediately, Rouletabille, understanding that Nicole's behavior and manner of speech had been commanded by prudence, continued to play his part. "I beg your pardon, Mademoiselle. I thought that there was no one in here." And he closed his door again, and went back to work as if nothing had happened.

Two minutes later, he saw the automobile drawing away with Helena, Nicole, Richter and the butler.

Bah! he thought. *I'll see her again at the engagement party!*

And they did meet again there.

When the day came, Rouletabille went to the Essener-Hoff with Richter himself, who was treating him entirely as a friend.

Rouletabille was not the only French reporter who had already visited the Essener-Hoff. Another great reporter, Jules Huret,[22] has given us this description of it:

The Krupp House—the Essener-Hoff—is a very curious place. With its double staircase with pink marble columns, with gilded copper banisters, it has a grandiose air. In the entrance hall, to either side of a vast stone fireplace, sculpted masks represent the human types of the five continents. The floor is covered with red tiles on which carpets are laid; sofas and armchairs upholstered in red leather are aligned along the walls. The house is principally intended to receive official envoys who have come to Essen to place orders for artillery.

They were treated as guests there, and treated royally. Some of those envoys remained there for a year, or even two years, to assist in the manufacture, with the result that, with its fifty rooms, the Essener-Hoff cost the factory something like 500,000 francs a year, not counting supplementary expenses.

At the moment that concerns us, there were, naturally, only representatives of powers allied with Germany, and a few neutral countries, in residence. There were also a few neutral journalists, carefully selected from the germanophilic press. In sum, the majority of the people

---

[22] Jules Huret (1853-1915) traveled extensively in the early years of the 20th century, sending back reports to *Le Figaro* and other Parisian newspapers from various parts of Europe and the Americas; he was the best-known of Leroux's colleagues and rivals. He published two books on Germany, in 1907 and 1913.

who had made up the Emperor's cortege during the nocturnal tour of the Krupp factory, had been invited by General von Berg.

The gala lunch was held in the large ballroom, and when Richter arrived with Rouletabille they found a large crowd there already, which was in an exceedingly cheerful mood. The ladies were wearing low necklines, as if for a dinner.

As he went through the drawing-rooms, Rouletabille had spotted Vladimir. When he went into the ballroom he saw Nicole. Then he looked for Princess Botosani, but could not see her. He was astonished that she had not been invited. Richter introduced the reporter to Nicole—he had already had the opportunity to introduce him to Helena.

"A compatriot," said Richter, in a loud voice. "It must be a great consolation for the two of you to encounter one another in this abominable country where prisoners are treated as slaves and allowed to die of starvation."

"Ach!" exclaimed General von Berg, behind them. "Monsieur Michel Talmar and Mademoiselle Nicole can obtain a few good provisions today, assuredly!"

And, bursting out into coarse laughter, he indicated the immense table already covered with the delicacies most appreciated by Teutonic palates, and pyramids of fruits, cakes and sweetmeats. "We lack for nothing! In truth, we lack for nothing!"

Nicole and Rouletabille did not have a chance to say anything to one another before the meal. The General introduced "the celebrated French engineer Michel Talmar" personally to the principal foreign guests, never failing to give details of his collaboration and partnership with Richter at the heart of the Krupp factory.

"There's an intelligent Frenchman," he concluded, "who truly understands his own interests. He hasn't gone to take his invention to England! He's been smarter than Fulbert!"

Coarse laughter greeted his allusion to the inventor's misfortune.

"Shh!" said the General then, with a broad smile full of malice. "We're making Mademoiselle Nicole uncomfortable. His Majesty confided her to me when he left."

Everyone looked at Nicole, who did not look at anyone—not even Rouletabille, who seemed to be plunged into a profound reverie.

Before they sat down at the table, Rouletabille and Nelpas Paha maneuvered so cleverly that they were able to obtain two minutes of conversation without attracting anyone's attention.

"You have what I asked you for?" asked Rouletabille.

Vladimir slipped a small phial into his hand. "Yes. Twenty drops will suffice for one person."

"Thanks...and the *Wesel*?"

"Bad news," Vladimir replied, between his teeth. "I've seen the captain of the *Wesel*; he's received orders to transport fifty Boche to Holland on his next trip."

"How many crewmen?" Rouletabille asked.

"Seven."

"Eight with the captain. After all, that only makes fifty-eight men."

"That's a lot," Vladimir observed, "for three fellows who might need to take possession of a vessel without making too much noise."

"Bah! No one will notice anything, and I hope that we won't need to take possession of anything at all."

"Damn it, I hope so!"

"What time are the crates arriving aboard the *Wesel*?" Rouletabille asked.

"Everything has to be loaded by six o'clock in the morning. The new timetable requires the ship to raise anchor at seven. Remember that your escape will be noticed by five at the latest. They can do a lot in two hours."

"Like what?"

"Capture you and take you back to the factory, for instance."

"That's quite possible," Rouletabille replied dryly, "But they'll only bring back corpses. By the way, my dear Pacha, how is Princess Botosani?"

He could not continue, though; they were sitting down at table. He was a long way from Vladimir and a long way from Nicole, between an aged *hauptmann* who boasted of being the factory's oldest employee, and a young *backfisch* for sixteen or eighteen, a cousin of Hans, who never stopped talking and telling Rouletabille in the greatest details about a week-long trip she had once made to Paris. It was a city she liked a great deal, because of Magic-City.[23]

"They say that the Emperor might destroy Paris," she said, by way of conclusion, but I hope we won't destroy Magic-City!"

The comment was heard and enjoyed great success. Von Berg began by declaring that Julius Caesar was on-

---

[23] Magic-City was a dance hall located in the Rue de l'Université. Leroux and the *backfisch* [girl] were not to know that, undestroyed by Zeppelin raids and Big Bertha shells, it would become notorious in the 1920s as the venue of an annual Mardi Gras "drag ball."

ly an imbecile by comparison with the Emperor, and that the Emperor would destroy anything he had to, even Magic-City, if necessary, in order that *Kultur* would triumph over the entire world.

"That is, moreover, what our friends—and, we can even add, after parading our gazes around this vast table, some of our enemies—have already began to understand very well."

At these last words, Rouletabille could not help blushing all the way to his earlobes. Nicole, for her part, did not blush at all, but she looked at Rouletabille, who looked at her. They both seemed to understand one another, and lowered their noses toward their plates.

The movement had undoubtedly been noticed by the brilliant assembly, for the brilliant assembly burst out in applause and cries of "Hoch!" and "Hurrah!"

The reporter was less concerned with his own shame and humiliation, which he hoped to be able to follow up soon with a striking vengeance, than the sentiments of rage and dolor that must be afflicting Nicole's heart.

He was grateful to the young woman for showing so much wisdom in the face of monsters who were mocking her and her country. Rouletabille had only to recall the outburst of fury that had concluded the last meeting of Nicole and Serge to estimate the cost of Fulbert's daughter's silence in the face of von Berg's last words.

She did not flinch. She was thus being obedient to him, Rouletabille, and proving that she had a confidence in him that, as we know, extended all the way to death. All the same, for a woman like her, it is easier to die than to hear it said that one has become a friend of the Boche without protest.

She deserves to be saved, the reporter swore to himself, *and I shall save her*.

At that moment, the aged *hauptmann* who was seated to his right leaned toward Rouletabille and said: "Admit that a great many nasty things have been said in your country about our Emperor—the world doesn't know who it's slandering. Do you know why His Majesty came to Essen recently? Because the rumor was beginning to run around the world that the inventor Fulbert's daughter had been maltreated here. He wanted to render account personally of the value of those rumors, and you can see with your own eyes how we're looking after the inventor Fulbert's daughter! Look, someone's pouring her more champagne—genuine French champagne, purchased in Reims, which can't do her any harm. Ach! The Emperor, you see, my dear Monsieur, if I may be forgiven for making use of an English term, is a perfect gentleman! Always a perfect gentleman! So, one would kill oneself for him. Me, I'm an old crock who's already set my bones marching three times, but he has only to give the sign, and I'd go back. My old carcass belongs to him! He's a perfect gentleman!"

"Could you pass me the red cabbage?" asked the young cousin on Rouletabille's left, "and pour me some sauce, and stop listening to that old bore who'll be telling us about his campaigns next. When you're seated near him at dinner your head aches as if someone had been using it as a dartboard for three days. Ach? All these people are too serious for a girl like me—a young *backfisch* who has been to Paris and knows how to appreciate *Franzosiche frivolitet*!"

Many other amicable or menacing things were said during the engagement meal. Fräulein Helena was radiant and the excellent Richter never ceased looking at her with eyes softened by the charm of a carnation and the good taste of a dress that was almost the same color as the carnation. Add blue ribbons to all that, and fasten it around the body of a goddess with a silver-buckled belt, decorated with little rhinestones, and you won't be at all astonished that the worthy Richter was in love.

We shall not waste time either in listing the numerous enormous dishes that were politely "cleared" during that little fête by guests rendered very joyful by the most highly-appreciated vintages of German and French wine, and also—it is necessary to be truthful—by the certainty of the imminent triumph of *kultur*.

From that viewpoint, the patriotic delirium was beginning to take on interesting proportions at dessert—which was, as is appropriate, a time for toasts. They were numerous, and full of a redoubtable spirit.

A regiment that came to parade before the windows of the banquet brought the general delight to a head, with the echo of the precise and heavy rhythm of a thousand boots hammering the soil of old Germany simultaneously; and as, almost immediately, hundreds of voices began intoning a flamboyant martial song, the guests joined in with *Am Rhein, am Rhein, Am Deutchen Rhein*—while, of course, raising their glasses with gestures imitative of the brandishing of sabers. The whole performance was terminated by roars of *Russen kaput! Englander kaput!* and a host of other *kaputs!* which inevitably included *Franzosen kaput!*

Rouletabille, red in the face, sank his fingernails into the palms of his hands, while looking anxiously at Nicole—who seemed a trifle agitated.

Then came the speeches, and more toasts...

Finally, they left the table and spread out into the drawing-rooms to take coffee and liqueurs and smoke horrid cigars.

That was the moment for which Rouletabille had been waiting in order to get close to Nicole. In the general hubbub, he was able to join her in the corner of a drawing-room and, slipping surreptitiously to her side, he gave her the little phial that Vladimir had brought and said: "Take this. There's enough to put your guard to sleep, and Helena, if necessary, and the entire Hans family. Twenty drops per person is sufficient. Put in thirty!"

Nicole looked at Rouletabille without making a movement.

"Put the phial in your pocket!"

"In a moment. People are looking at us. Have you anything more to tell me?"

"Yes."

"Then speak swiftly. We don't know whether we'll have another opportunity."

"Well," he said, "it's set for tonight, at three o'clock in the morning sharp. Leave the Hans house in Helena's clothes, mantle and hood. Go to Richter's house. If anyone catches sight of you, don't pay them any heed. An amorous rendezvous on the night of an engagement dinner isn't going to astonish anyone in Germany. Go up the steps; a window will open and you'll be lifted into the small workroom."

"Who'll take me in? You?"

"Me or someone else. I'll be very busy. Let yourself be guided; everything will be done under my orders. If you aren't there by three-thirty, it will be because something unexpected has prevented you from getting out of the Hans house. In that case, stay in your room. I'll come to look for you there."

179

"Are you sure it will succeed?"

"Oh yes."

"Because your promise still stands."

"Still."

Nicole smiled at Rouletabille.

Then, suddenly, the young man took on a waxen pallor, and left Nicole. He had to turn away in order to hide his visible disturbance, for he had just seen General von Berg looking at both of them attentively.

He avoided the general, because at that moment, the reporter might have found it impossible to say anything. His hesitant steps took him through the rejoicing crowd in search of Vladimir, and once he was close to the Slav again it was in such a changed voice that he spoke to him that Vladimir was immediately alarmed.

"What's happening?"

"Listen Vladimir, listen! Why isn't Princess Botosani here? Wasn't she invited?"

"Yes, of course she was invited!"

Rouletabille could not conceal a movement of joy, and the color returned to his cheeks. "Oh, my God!" he said. "My God! Is it possible? You're sure? You're sure of that?"

"Of what?"

"Of what you just told me—that Princes Botosani was invited."

"Absolutely. Not only did she tell me, but I saw the printed invitation."

"Heavens above! I'm coming back to life. Who sent out the invitations?"

"General von Berg himself."

"Thank you! You don't know how much good you've done me."

"But once again, what's happening? It seemed to be going so well a little while ago. I saw you talking to Nicole. She smiled as if she were with the angels."

"That's true," said Rouletabille, in a grave tone. "She smiled at me. Mark my words, Vladimir, that young woman is sublime. There's nothing in the world more beautiful or heroic than Nicole." He paused momentarily, and then added: "Now tell me why Princess Botosani, who as invited, hasn't come to the engagement party."

"Do you need to speak to her, then?"

"I don't know her," Rouletabille said, "And I don't want to know her. I don't have anything to say to her."

"No regrets then."

"Yes, al the same, I regret...I regret a great deal. But you haven't told me the reason for her absence. Is she ill, perhaps?"

"Not at all—but this morning, when she was trying on a magnificent dress, which would have made her the queen of the fête—for she always wants to be the star everywhere—she received orders to go to a business lunch where she was to meet a special envoy from Enver Pacha, a representative of the *Wilhelmstrasse* and another important person whose name she didn't want to give me."

Rouletabille's color had vanished again. "Strange!" he murmured. "A fatal coincidence!" And he passed his hand over his forehead, which was beaded with cold sweat.

He drew away from Vladimir and moved closer to Nicole. The latter perceived him, passed close to him and said to him: "I'm counting on you. I always keep my promises. Keep yours!" And she smiled once again, as one smiles at the angels.

Rouletabille let himself fall into a large leather arm-chair. He remained there, his head buried in his hands, for a few moments. Then he got up, and rejoined Vladimir in a shadowy corner where they were able to chat undisturbed for five minutes.

When they emerged from that shadow, they were both as pale as one another.

Nelpas Pacha went to salute von Berg, Helena and Richter, asking their permission to withdraw because he felt slightly indisposed. On considering the appearance of Enver Pacha's representative, the others had no difficulty in believing it. He therefore took his leave. As he was going through a small room that lead to the main staircase, he found himself face to face with Rouletabille between two doors.

"Embrace me!" the latter said to him. "We might never see one another again!"

Vladimir hugged him with even more emotion than in Paris.

"Say farewell to La Candeur!" said Vladimir, in a tearful voice, and, without looking back, launched himself toward the stairway.

"Poor La Candeur!" sighed Rouletabille, left alone. "I'm the one who brought him here!"

And with the tips of his fingers, he wiped away a large tear that was running down his cheek.

Then he went back to the drawing-rooms, where he soon astonished Richter himself by the great authority with which he explained to a few specialists his personal notions regarding the manufacture of sewing-machines...

Chapter XIX
To Be or Not to Be

Snow is falling in Essen. That is also part of the Inferno: cold. An icy night in Krupp's: a black and white
night; the black of whirlwinds of smoke, the white of
whirlwinds of snow. A furious wind mixes all of that
together. More than any other corner of the factory,
Richter's *kommando* disappears in that sinister mobile
white-stained shadow, for the buildings comprising it are
not aflame with the intermittent fulgurant gleams emerging from the crucibles and forges of the workshops of
war.

Behind the engineer's offices there is a small deserted courtyard, only used for the private and domestic
services of Richter and his family.

Suddenly, a window overlooking that courtyard
opens, and a shadow lets itself slip down on to the carpet
of snow, whose pallor is scarcely visible in the thick
darkness guarded by the high walls.

Is that living shadow the shadow of a man or an animal? Like the shadow of a dog, it walks on all fours
through the snow. It goes back and forth along the wall,
seemingly sniffing the ground like a hunting dog scent-
ing a trail. Then it stands up beside the wall. It is definitely a human shadow.

A rope is thrown over the wall by the man, and
must be fitted with a grappling-iron that has hooked on
to some projection, or some significantly-pierced iron
bar, for at the first tug, the rope does not yield to the

hand pulling it, and supports the body that immediately makes use of it to climb.

The wall is old, and beneath the agile feet that use it as a point of support, a few small stones are detached and fall into the snow. Undoubtedly, however, the shadow does not think that depredation sufficient, for as soon as it arrives at the crest of the wall, it detaches a few more fragments, which fall inside and outside the courtyard. Then the shadow disappears outside the enclosure, after having thrown the rope down on the other side of the wall.

A few minutes go by.

Now the rope is thrown down into the courtyard again and the shadow, returning, lets itself slide down to the ground. After making a few bizarre gestures, the man becomes an animal again, and returns on all fours to the window from which it emerged, but moving backwards.

Having arrived at that window, it goes back into the Richter house. It bumps into another shadow, which asks it: "Do you still need my shoes? Damn it, I'm shivering...and for our affair, it's necessary not to catch a cold in the head!"

"Here are your boots—stop complaining," says Rouletabille, freeing his hands from the enormous shoes into which they had been inserted, and which he has used to create, in the snow, in company with his own, a visible trail, with the evident intention of fostering the belief that a small group of runaways has taken a route that the young people obviously have no intention of following.

"What about the warehouse supervisor?" asks Rouletabille, in a whisper, while working with a pick, which he is using as a master key to force a door very gently—an operation doubtless necessary to create belief in a false trail.

"The warehouse supervisor?" La Candeur repeats while putting his shoes on again with a broad smile of satisfaction. "Bah—he won't give us away."

"You've killed Lasker?"

"I had to. He found my with the crates, and was too interested in what I was doing—asked me questions that worried me…worried me so much, old chap, that I was obliged to make triply certain that he'd never question me again! I've had a sprained wrist since the fireman-sergeant, you know?"

"And where did you put the body?"

"Exactly! I don't know what to do with it—inspiration isn't my strong suit. For the time being, I hid it under a pile of waste paper."

"But they'll find it right away, idiot! You say that Lasker won't give us away—you didn't think that his corpse will give us away! And we'll be captured before we get out of the warehouse."

"Damn it! What shall we do, then?"

"Listen—this is what you're going to do. Take another sewing-machine out of its crate and replace it in the stack of those that aren't yet ready to be packed. Then put Lasker's body in the crate. He'll escape with us!"

"Understood—and right away!" whispered La Candeur, about to carry out the order he had just received.

Rouletabille stopped him. "One moment! Don't go without telling me where you put the firemen's uniforms and caps."

"Over there, in the wooden box."

"Go!"

La Candeur's shadow disappeared into a corridor, and in spite of the shadow being shod this time in the huge boots, it made no more sound than when gliding in socks; the habit of the reportage, as dangerous as it was exceptional, accomplished by La Candeur in Rouletabille's company had given the latter a great discretion of movement.

In the meantime, Rouletabille finished the task that he knew to be necessary to the security of their departure; nothing had been neglected to make sure that the consequent search would go astray.

When La Candeur came back and announced that Lasker's body was suitably packed, Rouletabille was in the process of putting on one of the firemen's uniforms. The reporter struck a match and looked at his watch.

"It's time!" he said. He rolled up the other uniforms under his arm. "Listen carefully to what I'm going to tell you. I'll leave the Richter house by the front door. You stay in the design-studio. No one ever goes there, especially by night. Only Richter can get in, but after today's little party he'll be sleeping profoundly, like everyone else."

"All the same, what if he comes?"

"If he comes, kill him."

"Understood—but what with? My wrist's injured."

"With this," said Rouletabille, going to his small work-room, from which he returned with a heavy lever terminated by a sold mass, which made the steel bar into a redoubtable hammer. Momentarily, the moon illuminated the weapon, which was set down within La Candeur's reach on a drawing-board.

"Look—the moon's rising!" La Candeur remarked. "One can see clearly enough to work."

The star was immediately veiled, however. The wind that had not ceased blowing had, however, cleared the lugubrious night of some of its swirling smoke and chased away the storm-clouds.

"Don't budge from this spot until you see a shadow appear on the steps. I'll leave you Richter's key. Open the door to that shadow—you'll recognize it; it will be Nicole, in Helena's clothes and headgear. Bring her in and say to her: 'Rouletabille will come!' That's all, understand? No noise, no unnecessary chat. You have nothing else to say to her. If she questions you, you won't reply. Understood?"

"Understood. But what if she doesn't come?"

"If she isn't here when I get back, it's agreed that I'll go to find her—but you don't budge."

"All right!"

"Obey, and nothing more. Since you're devoid of inspiration, don't imagine that you should do things that might seem ordinary to you but might have terrible consequences!"

"I'll obey like a brute."

"Adieu!"

"Adieu."

They embraced, for La Candeur judged from Rouletabille's quivering that they were reaching a critical point in the drama, even though he did not understand the plot. He knew some things, but there were others he did not know, and what he did not know appeared to him to be an abyss just as profound as, and even more redoubtable than, the night whose depths contained all the mystery of the Krupp factory.

Rouletabille left. La Candeur sat down and waited.

He waited for half an hour. Then the expected shadow arrived. It was standing on the steps.

La Candeur opened the door to it.

It recoiled slightly on perceiving the enormous shadow of La Candeur, who immediately whispered: "Rouletabille will come!"

Then it came into the house and into the design-studio, sat down in the usual place and whispered: "Will he come soon?"

La Candeur, faithful to his instructions, pretended that he had not heard and went to sit down on the far side of the rom.

Undoubtedly Nicole understood that it was preferable to maintain a perfect silence, for she did not ask any more questions. From time to time she turned her head toward the small office, through the window of which an occasional ray of moonlight illuminated her beautiful, sad and dolorous profile.

A few sighs, alive with the anguish of her agitated soul, escaped her.

Finally, Rouletabille appeared on the steps in his turn. He was not alone. He had two other firemen with him. All three moved rapidly into the design-studio.

The other two were Serge Kaniewsky and Fulbert.

"God be praised, Mademoiselle, since you're here," said Rouletabille. "We don't have a second to waste, and a few minutes' delay on your part could have compromised everything..."

As he pronounced these last words, a glance darted through the window of the small workroom allowed him to perceive a number of disquieting shadows advancing through the quarter, which was normally deserted at this hour. Thus, it was in a feverish fashion that he interrupted the commencement of the delight that had taken possession of Serge as soon as the latter had perceived Nicole's silhouette, and ordered the Pole and Fulbert to follow his friend—La Candeur—and do everything that he told them to do.

As Serge and Fulbert hesitated to draw away from Nicole, Rouletabille whispered: "We'll follow you! Go, or we're doomed!" Turning to Nicole, he hissed between his teeth: "Order them to obey!"

Nicole did not say a word, but she pushed Serge ahead of her with a brutal gesture.

La Candeur was already dragging Fulbert and Serge away, but Rouletabille was no longer looking in that direction. All his attention went to the window of the work-room, through which he was alarmed to see military silhouettes everywhere, which were surrounding this corner of Richter's *kommando* with a veritable cordon, which as tightening by the second.

Nicole had seen them too, and her finger pointed at the menacing shadows while her mouth croaked: "Too late! We're doomed!"

Did Rouletabille believe it?

Did he, too, think that all was lost? Or that his hope of saving Nicole was too faint to run the risk of leaving her alive in the hands of the torturers of his race—a formidable gamble on which the salvation of the fatherland might perhaps depend?

At any rate, his hand went in search, behind him, of the heavy lever that he had deposited there—and then, silently, and doubtless also in order that the noble young woman who had already suffered so much would not see the death that she had commanded herself coming, covertly, he struck her.

He struck her on the head.

He struck with all his strength, but—O horror!—the unfortunate woman did not fall under the furious blow.

She turned around, clutched at a curtain, and uttered a frightful groan.

Rouletabille had to repeat the blow, and she fell to her knees, mouth open, eyes very wide, fixing her murderer with the stare of a fatally-wounded animal—a stare that the other would never forget.

Finally, after a final and futile effort, which brought her upright in the fact of the supreme blow, she fell to the floor, and was no more than a poor mere object, inert in the icy rays of moonlight.

Trembling with horror, Rouletabille still had his weapon in his hand when La Candeur appeared. The giant recoiled before the frightful face of his comrade, before the gesture that was still menacing, as if he had not struck enough, and before the body of the woman that blocked his way.

At the same time, the moonlight was interrupted by a rush of shadows that precipitated itself on to the steps, and silhouettes agitating outside the widow.

"Pick up the corpse," said Rouletabille, in a voice that La Candeur did not recognize, so altered was it.

The other obeyed without taking account of what he was doing.

Almost at the same instant as the door closed behind the two men and their sinister burden, other doors gave way under the furious pressure of military shadows, which were waving lanterns and uttering savage cries—and immediately, the shadows and the lanterns went astray on the false trail prepared by the reporter's audacious cunning.

Chapter XX
In the Depths of the Hold

The *Wesel*, a cargo-ship transporting merchandise between Duisburg and Holland, is still at the dock, but is making ready to sail up the Rhine.

In the silent darkness below decks, pierced by the unique and precise light of a lantern, a sudden creaking is audible—and as if the sound, in that mute night, were astonished by itself, it stops immediately...and then begins again, but this time more hesitantly, so uncertain, and fearful of echoes that it ends up dying away softly, its force exhausted.

Finally, all of a sudden, there is a brutal and angry eruption. Planks are hurled away, and from a smashed create, a body rolls into the bloody light of the lantern, which is swaying between two inclined joists.

Then another body rolls out. The two bodies are alive. The space available for their movements is not large enough for them to have been heard up above; so, having abruptly got up on to their knees, they find themselves face to face with one another, like the bodies of two animals with snorting muzzles, breathless and hostile.

One of the muzzles asks: "Nicole?" But the other only replies with heavy breathing.

Serge Kaniewsky and Rouletabille are face to face with one another, in the depths of the *Wesel*'s hold—in the depths of the abyss...

"Nicole?" repeats the grunting voice of the Pole. "Where's Nicole?"

"In one of these crates," Rouletabille whispers.

"But which one? Which? Which? Perhaps she's fainted. Perhaps she's dead? Why isn't she giving any sign of life? Why?"

"The crates have been separated from one another. Wait a moment...patience and composure. Perhaps our companions aren't even in this hold. Those crates have been left on the deck..."

"You swore to me that we wouldn't be separated!"

"Who says that we've been separated?" replied Rouletabille's lugubrious voice. "We're all aboard. We'll find one another eventually."

But the Pole's fever only increased. He was turning around in the narrow space like a hyena in its cage...and he came back to Rouletabille, showing his teeth as if he could no longer hold back from devouring him.

"Silence!" commanded the reporter. "I think something moved in this direction..." And he plunged into the darkness.

In the depths of the night, his voice was heard prudently calling out to La Candeur and Fulbert.

The Pole soon caught up with him.

"Why? Why aren't you calling to Nicole." And Serge implored: "Nicole! Nicole!"

But only silence replied to those desperate appeals.

"She's dead!" croaked the Pole. "Otherwise she'd already have heard my voice! Oh, I was right not to want to allow myself to be shut up in the crate without her! But if she's dead, I'll kill you all! All of you!"

"You can do as you wish," Rouletabille whispered. "Me, I've done what I could!"

"Tell me, then that you've saved her, if you don't want to die here and now." And the Pole, who seemed to be at the end of his tether, backed Rouletabille into a corner as if he wanted to tear him to pieces.

Rouletabille pushed away the muzzle of the man who was sending fiery breath into his face—which only redoubled the other's rage.

"Ah!" grated the Pole, whose fangs gripped Rouletabille's cravat. "Tell me, then, that you've saved her. Tell me that—or I swear that you're finished!"

Then the reporter, having shaken off the malevolent beast again, came back to a position directly underneath the light of the lantern, and there, squatting on his heels, with his chin in his hands, said: "I repeat that I've done everything I could to save her."

"That's not...that's not what you promised me! If you value your skin, I need to see Nicole!"

"I don't value my skin, but you shall see Nicole."

"Ah!" moaned the other, exhausted by rage, impotence and crazed anguish, "if she were saved, you wouldn't be talking to me like that. She's dead! She's dead! Bane of my life! She's dead and we're alive!"

This time, Rouletabille made no reply. He searched, at the bottom of one of his pockets, for a piece of paper, unfolded it slowly and gave it to the Pole.

Serge took the piece of paper mechanically. He did not understand.

"Read!"

And the Pole, by the red light of the lantern, read it.

When he had finished reading what was written on the piece of paper, and took cognizance of the blank check given to the criminal by the victim herself, there was no further cry, nor a sigh, nor a groan, nor anything at all. The head of the man fell, and hit the deck with a dull thud.

Rouletabille tried in vain to reanimate the inert body. The life of the man had been so intimately linked with Nicole's that the very idea of Nicole's death had effectively knocked Serge unconscious. To bring him out of it required nothing less than the icy water of a bottle for which the reporter went to search in the crate, and, most of all, an unexpected phrase whispered in his ear:

"She might not be dead!"

The man moved, sighed, and opened his eyes again.

The furious passage of life into near-oblivion determined a few moments before by the mere idea of the death of his beloved had been foreseen by Rouletabille, and the brutality of his action had been calculated, in the hope of obtaining explanations whose possibility he would have had to renounce without that knock-out blow.

However, the reporter too was at the end of his tether. His task was accomplished. Whatever happened now, the Boches would never obtain the secrets of a man who no longer had the opportunity to give them away. If the affair turned bad, Rouletabille would die with Serge, for he would not hesitate to strike him, any more than he had hesitated in that tragic moment when he had created a corpse in the near-darkness of the design-studio.

Strengthened by having thus succeeded, without weakness, in depriving the *Titania* of the soul that it needed in order to live fully, but weakened by all the effort expended, and also moved by the desolate dolor of the man who was listening to him as a dying man listens to the words that might reattach him to life, Rouletabille—indifferent henceforth so far as he was concerned to the consequences of a promise that might have been fatal to him—admitted that he had struck Nicole dead, *because he was not sure that it had been Nicole!*

He related the circumstance as one reads a report, in a blank and monotonous voice to which as added, without him suspecting it, the horror of a crime rendered necessary, not by any certainty, but by an absolute doubt. For doubt too, is a conclusion, like affirmation or negation, and leads in certain circumstances to a pitiless verdict.

He began by explaining how he had witnessed the famous interview between Serge and Fulbert's daughter and what had followed it, and how Nicole had been led to sign the paper that gave him the right of life or death over her.

Then there was the young woman's prolonged absence; Rouletabille's anxiety; his nocturnal visit to the Hans house, before Nicole's window...and then Nicole's futile return to Richter's office in the company of Helena...and finally, the engagement party.

It was there that the drama had undergone a sudden twist.

Momentarily, Rouletabille had wondered whether he was really confronted by Fulbert's daughter. By that time, however, he had already pronounced the words that advertised the flight and indicated the rendezvous in Richter's offices.

That explained the reporter's sudden pallor and distress in the Essener-Hoff. Already, for several minutes, he had been astonished by certain attitudes and mannerisms on Nicole's part that were scarcely appropriate to her. The young woman's calmness, her passivity in the face of the brutally patriotic manifestations of General von Berg's guests, had appeared to him to be almost inexplicable, given the memory of the vengeful exaltation that had previously excited Serge's fiancée, in spite of all prudence, during her interview with the Pole.

That Rouletabille had at first attributed that unexpected reserve to heroism had been necessary, but during the subsequent conversation he had had with the young woman, the latter had smiled so singularly when he had reminded her of his promise, that Rouletabille had had the sharp impression that she was utterly ignorant of the nature of that promise! People smiled in that fashion when reminded of a contract of love, but not a contract of death!

And if, on turning round under the shock caused by that incredible smile, Rouletabille had not perceived General von Berg staring at them so assiduously, the reporter would have been almost certain that he had just been speaking to someone other than Nicole! But what was going on? That smile was not required by the comedy that Nicole had to play under excessively curious gazes...

Inexpressible anguish! Indescribable anxiety! Prescience of a supreme deception by an enemy that needed, in order to carry through its blackmail, a healthy Nicole, while the other one, the true one, was doubtless, at that moment, dead or dying!

That deception was all the easier to imagine and to execute because they only had to display the false Nicole at a distance, and rapidly, to a man who was burning with fever behind a window-pane. It was less a matter of finding an exact resemblance than a silhouette of approximate conformity.

The Nicole who was exhibited at the party at the Essener-Hoff was unknown to those who were not the artisans of the redoubtable comedy, as was Fulbert's real daughter. There was no one but Rouletabille who could form suspicions! And even he...

Rouletabille, it is necessary to remember, only knew Nicole very slightly. He had only seen her at close range once, in the semi-darkness of his work-room, when she had been thrown in there by von Berg, and in circumstances so dramatic that he could not remember he details exactly enough not to be deceived by a resemblance. As for the voice, he had only exchanged a few rapid words with her.

Finally, to corroborate Rouletabille's doubts, there was Nicole's last visit to Richter's house, when the young woman, left alone in the design-studio, had not even turned her head in the direction of Rouletabille's work-room and had started at the latter's appearance like someone taken by surprise, who had no idea that the room might be occupied. Had that, again, been a comedy designed to deceive others than Rouletabille? The young man no longer thought so, after the smile at the engagement party.

At any rate, the reporter had the duty to doubt. In the face of that duty to doubt, he considered his duty to act. The Nicole to whom he had spoken, true or false, only knew the time and place of his escape plan, but did not know the means of escape. In any case, she would come to the rendezvous punctually—all the more so if she was an impostor—in order to find out more. Doubtless she would have taken her precautions and warned those who needed to know; doubtless, in collaboration with her, a trap would have been prepared. It was up to Rouletabille to avoid it.

In consequence of which, the reporter had prepared a false trail himself, which, if necessary, would lead the police dogs launched after the fugitives astray for a few minutes. When the moment to act arrived, we know how, at that precise moment, shadows had surged forth from all directions—which had not surprised the reporter in the least, but which had added further mass to the pan of the balance in which Rouletabille was in the process of weighing the fake Nicole. Nevertheless, the reporter's mind retained too much lucidity to give the value of proof to that redoubtable intervention. The police might have been there, and might have discovered Rouletabille secrets, without Nicole having given them away. And since the reporter had not had time, in view of the rapidity of events, to establish the real identity of the young woman with the aid of her father and her fiancé, he had struck her without knowing exactly who it was that he was striking, because it was his duty to strike—and because he had received, from the very hand of the true Nicole, the order to strike!

It would be difficult to give to that cold summary of a chain of reasoning that only Rouletabille was capable of conceiving, the icy and fatal color that forged its originality in the depths of the abysm where a great passion was seething. A professor, armed with a stick of chalk, could not have traced in a calmer and more detached fashion the analysis of an algebraic equation on a blackboard, to the end of which he added the fateful letters Q. E. D.

The reporter had no sooner fallen silent, however, than sinister groans emerged from the shadows, and Serge's slavering and barking voice filed it with incoherent syllables. Rouletabille raised his head and saw, facing him, eyes of fire—the eyes of a wolf when wolves are avid for human flesh.

In spite of his composure, he could not sustain the bloody glare of those eyes, and he turned away.

Then he saw two other eyes, less fiery, but so terribly ad that they frightened him even more than the first. At the same time he heard Fulbert's voice saying: "And now, how are we ever going to know whether it was my daughter that you killed?"

Chapter XXI
Dead or Alive?

"We have the body here," said Rouletabille.

"And you're talking!" Serge cried.

Rouletabille put his hand over the Pole's quivering muzzle.

"I'm not taking as loudly as you, at any rate! Stop howling and despairing...all is not lost, Serge Kaniewsky."

"How can you say, madman, that all is not lost? If the body isn't Nicole's it's because Nicole in still in their hands...and she'll have to pay for all of us! But you'll be the first to pay for her, I swear!"

They fell silent, because of a frightful groan that came from the side. That groan said: "I've been forced to travel with my daughter's corpse! There was a corpse beside me! In the same crate as me! A cadaver separated from me by wooden spars, whose clothing I touched. Come with me to tear the spars away. We're both cursed because of you, Serge! Tear away the spars! Tear away the spars! Afterwards, we'll make a new coffin for Nicole...an astonishing coffin, worthy of her, as big as the *Titania*!"

The unfortunate man was raving, clutching at all the spars and shaking them like a madman, but Serge and Rouletabille soon ripped the pieces of wood away from the crate that had transported the old man—and, indeed, they pulled out a cadaver, which the Pole dragged, howling, into the light of the red lantern.

"It's the body of Lasker, the warehouse supervisor," said Rouletabille.

The Pole and Fulbert crouched over the body, like wild beasts sniffing it.

"The other body. We need the other body in order to know. We want the other body!"

"My companion is the only one who can tell you where it is," said Rouletabille, "and I don't know where my companion is."

At that moment, the shadows moved again, as if the darkness were being jostled by the passage of something enormous.

"Is that you, La Candeur?"

"Yes, it's me. I thought I'd never be able to find you. My crate's at the far end of the hold."

"The body! The body!" yapped the two furious voices.

"These Messieurs," Rouletabille said, "want to know where Nicole's body is. What have you done with it, La Candeur?"

"I didn't have time to carry it away, old chap—I left it behind."

Horrible growls full of menace greeted these words, although Fulbert's expiring voice still had the strength to say: "My God! We'll never know!"

"Yes!" said Rouletabille. "We'll soon know! Take my word for it—believe me!"

"When?"

"Soon?"

"When?"

"Soon. Perhaps in an hour, perhaps right away."

"Right away!" barked the Pole. "Right away! I can't wait!"

"Me neither," moaned the unfortunate Fulbert—and filled the hold with his sobbing.

"Silence!" Rouletabille commanded. "Listen! Didn't you hear the footsteps? If you continue moaning like that, you'll bring the entire crew down here—and it's not the crew that I'm expecting."

"Who are you expecting?" Fulbert moaned.

"I'm expecting someone who'll tell us the truth…for it's still necessary to have hope in the truth. Listen to me again for I haven't told you everything. Perhaps she's dead! She is dead! That's what it's necessary to say first, and that's what I'm telling you first…for after all, she might be dead! She is! Tell yourselves that, and curse me! And now, hope for a miracle, because…because I'm waiting for it, that miracle! I thought just now that I heard footsteps. Know that I had an accomplice in Essen…the so-called representative of Turkish interests."

"Vladimir! Vladimir!" sighed La Candeur. "Where's Vladimir?"

"It's him that I'm expecting. He's booked a passage on the boat—and I saw Vladimir at the Essener-Hoff, at the engagement party. I gave him a mission. Has he accomplished it? Everything depends on that—everything! When I perceived, or when I thought I perceived, at the engagement party, that Nicole wasn't Nicole…the sharp memory came back to my mind of certain words I'd heard spoken one night. That night, when I was on the roof of the Hans house, in the central research building, I overheard a few words pronounced by the guard who was in charge of guarding Nicole. He was congratulating himself because, in a few days' time he'd enjoy an appreciable liberty. 'After Wednesday,' he said. 'I was pretty sure that I'd be rid of it all…yes, we all thought here that it was finished…and over there, Princess Botosani said; *she'll be dead tomorrow*,' the guardsman added. Then there was a pause, and the man went on, without hiding his astonishment: 'And now, she's much better! It's incredible how resilient these young women are—not to mention that when they want her to look well, they can feed her an uncommon elixir.'

"Now," Rouletabille went on, "I knew that Princess Botosani was a volunteer nurse at the hospital in the Villa Hoegel, outside the factory, in Essen itself. Thus, they had transported poor Nicole to that hospital, fearing a dire outcome. Had she really come back? That was the whole question. The Boche had to great an interest in substituting a double for the possibility of such an eventuality not to occur to me, especially when I came to be assailed by the sharpest doubts about the true identity of the Nicole I had before me.

"It was then that I went to my accomplice Vladimir, who was in constant communication with Princess Botosani and asked him why the Princess wasn't at the engagement party. When he told me that the Princess had been invited to the party I breathed more easily, for it surely followed from that information that the Nicole I had before me was the true one. Princess Botosani had looked after her, and would never have been invited to the party, where she would have met Monsieur Fulbert's daughter, if she hadn't been the same person she had looked after. The princess would have seen through the deception immediately and would have immediately told her false Pacha, Vladimir, with whom she was known to be intimate. That would let too many people in on the secret, and it would also, however little doubt the guests at the Essener-Hoff might have about Nicole's identity, be contrary to the desires of the Emperor, who was determined that Monsieur Fulbert's daughter should be shown off in the flesh and in good health.

"I concluded, therefore, that the invitation to the Princess Botosani was a serious argument in favor of the real identity of the Nicole to whom I had just talked. However, when Vladimir had added that the invitation had been annulled by the necessity imposed upon the Princess of being unable to answer the invitation, all my doubts came back again, more urgent than ever. I was able to believe, or, at any rate, able to dread, that we had all been deceived...and I resolved to act as if we were in a desperate situation.

"It was then that I confided to Vladimir in great secrecy the dilemma in which we were henceforth struggling. He was free! He could act! And I told him what to do. He was to go to the hospital in the Villa Hoegel and personally make sure of what had happened there. It was on a Wednesday that the invalid had been taken to the hospital. She had been cared for by the Princess. Those were precious clues. Vladimir received orders to make contact, at all costs, with the invalid, if she was still in the hospital, and to use any means at his disposal, including Princess Botosani's automobile and papers, to get the invalid to the Dutch frontier and get her to safety before coming back to the *Wesel*, where his passage had been booked in advance.

"Messieurs, Vladimir is aboard the Wesel! He's watching over us and our enterprise, and we might see him appear at any moment! You see that nothing is lost! He's the one who will enlighten us! So long as he has not spoken, we should not despair!"

At that moment, a new person appeared in the red light of the lantern. He called out in a low voice: "Rouletabille! Rouletabille!"

"Is that you, Vladimir?"

"Yes, it's me."

"Well, did you save the invalid?"

"Yes."

"You've saved her?"

"Yes."

"She's safe in Holland?"

"Yes."

"Nicole Fulbert is safe, then!"

"But I don't know myself. I don't know whether the invalid is Nicole Fulbert."

"What are you saying? What are you saying? You've seen her."

"No, I didn't see her. She didn't show her face."

"And you saved her?"

"Yes, I saved, at any rate, the invalid who had been brought to the hospital on the Wednesday and had been care for by Princess Botosani."

"But after all, she must have told you her name!"

"She told me that her name is Barbara Lixte."

Chapter XXII
The Last Voyage of the Wesel

The rumor in the depths of the hold, and the rage, the entire hubbub of frantic sentiments that enveloped Rouletabille thwarted him again momentarily—momentarily!

How much longer would he be able to hold back those madmen, whom the prospect of Nicole's death was rendering increasingly intractable. But he was hanging on so grimly to the words emerging from Vladimir's mouth that he was no longer paying any heed to all the fury that was seething behind him, and digging its claws into him.

"Speak, Vladimir, speak! If she didn't tell you anything, perhaps it's because she couldn't tell you anything. We have to assume that, since it was necessary to substitute a healthy Nicole for the ailing Nicole, they were obliged to impose on the ailing Nicole another identity than her real one! Of course! Understand! And hope! Still hope! That other identity must have been imposed upon her on pain of death—and on pain of her father and fiancé being tortured. Always Boche blackmail! On every page, every line of the history of the world! Did you tell her, Vladimir, that you had come on behalf of Rouletabille?"

"I didn't dare!" Vladimir said. "I wasn't sure who the person in front of me was. She was so suspicious of me that I had to be suspicious too! She consented to be taken to Holland—that was already a great deal."

"Nothing is lost! Nothing is lost! But it's unfortunate that you weren't able to see her...for, after all, you'd seen the other Nicole at the engagement party, and if the Nicole in the hospital had resembled her, she would surely have been the real Nicole...for they needed a healthy Nicole and they had no reason to invent a sick one."

"It happened at night, and in the darkness of the ward and the courtyard of the hospital...and I only just had time to put the veiled woman into the Princess's automobile, and then I jumped into the driving-seat. I drove it myself. All in all, she didn't want to be seen...I think it was her...but I can't be sure of it, since I didn't know her. I can only tell you what she told me, and she told me that her name was Barbara Lixte, the woman captured in Germany and accused of the espionage of the famous Dutch democrat journalist. And that's why she agreed to flee to Holland with me...but as Barbara Lixte!"

"She did the right thing! She did the right thing! Since you were ready to take her away, at any price, and, even if you were setting a trap for her, she would benefit from that escape if she could...if she could...without, in case of mishap, the Boche being able to reproach her for having revealed her true identity. Nothing is lost! Nothing is lost! Let's hope! I tell you that we have the duty to hope! Do you hear, you two? Have you finished growling like that? Devouring me like that, with your eyes of fire? When you'd devoured me you wouldn't be any further forward! Vladimir! Where did you take the woman in Holland? Where is she waiting for us? For she is waiting for us, isn't she? You told her that she had to wait for us?"

"I only just had time to tell her that and come back. She's waiting for us at Arnhem, in the United Provinces Hotel. I told her to stay there until tomorrow morning."

"I tell you that everything is saved!" sighed Rouletabille. "We'll be in Arnhem before this evening. And there, we'll find Nicole!"

"If we don't find her," said the voice of the Pole, "you're dead!"

"Understood, understood! But first, my dear Monsieur, let's calm down and stay alert; and let's be prudent, circumspect and ready for anything—for the main thing, evidently, is to get to Arnhem."

At that moment, the muffled and repetitive sound of artillery-fire caused Rouletabille, La Candeur and Vladimir to prick up their ears...and all of a sudden, the Pole's rage and Fulbert's despair seemed to be suspended.

"What's that?" said Rouletabille. "But first of all, why haven't we got under way? By this time, we ought to be *en route*."

"I'll go and see," said Vladimir.

The Slav slid between the crates and disappeared.

He was gone for about ten minutes, during which the cannon fire did not stop. Rouletabille had difficulty suppressing his anxiety. The other two said nothing.

Finally, Vladimir reappeared. "It's quite simple," he said. "Your escape from the factory has been perceived, and they must suspect that you're aboard a boat, for the harbor has been closed and all departures suspended."

"Damn it! We're trapped again," groaned La Candeur. "It was all going so well!" La Candeur, who had made the sacrifice of Nicole a long time ago, though that all would be well as soon as they reached neutral territory.

Rouletabille simply said: "We'll leave all the same, because we have to leave. Are you ready, Vladimir?"

"I'm only ready for lunch at noon, myself," Vladimir replied.

"A Boche," the other replied, "is always ready to celebrate, at any time of the day or night—so take advantage of the forced delay in the work imposed by the official ban to get a party going. Get all the food out, and Nelpas Pacha's hampers of champagne! A Pacha, a friend of Enver the Magnificent, knows how to do things properly."

"Understood! All agreed for noon!"

"Let the feast begin. Go find the captain. To table— and quickly!"

"The captain does whatever I want," said Vladimir. "Nelpas Pacha is rich enough for that. And once the Messieurs have drunk, the rest won't be far behind. The champagne's a good vintage, I assure you."

"Send down the weapons quickly. We have to be masters of the boat in an hour. Offer them all a drink! Stuff them! In half an hour, we'll serve powder to anyone who hasn't drunk enough. And in a few hours, Messieurs, we'll be in Arnhem."

"Damn it!" La Candeur exclaimed again, in whom hope as reborn. "That's a last adventure I like—on condition, my dear Vladimir, that when you send down the weapons, you bring me a few bottles of champagne. I'm thirsty!"

"No, Vladimir replied. "It's better that you don't drink that champagne!"

You will certainly not have forgotten the dispatch published by all the Allied newspapers, sent from Le Havre on 15 January 1915. It recounted the extraordinary escape of a number of Liégeois, who had taken possession of a boat and had succeeded in fleeing by that means to Holland. Rouletabille related much later that he had been inspired by that dispatch in the plan he had made with Vladimir, and we can do no better than reproduce it here exactly:

Le Havre, 14 January

We were recently informed of an audacious coup by Belgians who, after having got some German mariners drunk, took possession of their boat and set a course for Holland, where they arrived without incident. That feat has just been repeated in extraordinary conditions of audacity. It has permitted three hundred Liégeois,[24] among whom were a number of women and children, to leave Liège by night aboard a boat requisitioned by the Germans, the Atlas V, *and to reach Holland.*

The Atlas V *is a tug, a former warship of a certain strength, subsequently bought by a neutral power. It left Liège at about midnight, carried by the strong current of the Meuse, which had been caused to overflow by flooding; in the course of its journey it encountered numerous obstacles: a wooden bridge near Visé, and cables laid across the river, but it overcame them all.*

The pilot had armored his cabin with the aid of steel plates taken from the coal-bunker. Thanks to that, he was able to brave numerous rifle-shots fired by German sentries and machine-gun fire. Cannon were even aimed at the vessel, but they could not reach it.

---

[24] In fact, there were only 107 people aboard the *Atlas V* when it made the historic journey in question on the night of 3-4 January 1914.

The voyage from Liège to Eisden in Holland was complete in an hour and three-quarters. The passengers were lying at the bottom of the hold. None was hit. We should add that the boat had just been repaired by the Germans at a cost of 3500 francs.

Things happened with similar simplicity aboard the *Wesel*. In the course of a lunch offered to the ship's officers, a part of the crew and fifty additional passengers, five demons, armed to the teeth, surged forth while the champagne was flowing freely and had already produced quite unexpected soporific effects on a certain number. The officers were taken prisoner and locked in the hold. The rest offered no resistance. The chief engineers and the mechanics had o obey the orders given to them under threat of death, and the *Wesel*, emerging from Duisburg, had soon reached Ruhrort, at the confluence of the Ruhr and the Rhine. It was there that difficulties might have faced the audacious fugitives, until then invincible. Pursued by a tug on the poop-deck of which numerous officers could be distinguished uttering veritable howls of rage, Rouletabille and his companions did not hesitate to open fire with all their weapons. The tug was soon joined by two motor launches.

Fortunately for our friends, an escape as extraordinary as that of a cargo-vessel defying official orders in the heart of Germany, in a region far from the hostilities, had not been anticipated. They found themselves disarmed before such audacity. There were plenty of gunboats along the Ruhr, but none was in a condition to give chase; they had returned there for repairs. The boats that gave chase to the *Wesel* were unarmed.

Sheltered behind the bulwarks and the sides, Rouletabille, Fulbert and the Pole shot numerous victims, while La Candeur and Vladimir watched over the captive crew and the stokers below decks, revolvers in hand.

North of Ruhrort, the pursuit was abandoned by the Boche, but Rouletabille did not think that it would be for long. The telephone must have done its work. They must have been warned at the frontier—but it was necessary to get through all the same.

They were ready for anything—to blow the boat up or scuttle it—if they could not get through.

The boilers were heated to the maximum. The entire hull of the *Wesel* was shuddering. And when, a kilometer from the frontier, the Boche vessels presented themselves, blocking the route, they went through the blockade—literally through it, for they sank one vessel, and were hit by a hail of machine-gun fire and ten shells…but they arrived in Holland. They arrived crippled, but they arrived!

A shell had blown the captain, his first mate and three sailors to smithereens, but as for the five passengers who are of interest to us, they were safe and sound, without a scratch.

Two hours later, Rouletabille and his acolytes, having explained the situation to the Dutch authorities, arrived in Arnhem, at the United Provinces Hotel, and immediately asked to see Madame Barbara Lixte.

They received the reply: "Madame Barbara Lixte let this morning for Rotterdam with her husband, who had come to fetch her."

Chapter XXIII
Barbara or Nicole?

They left for Rotterdam that same evening, and arrived there the following morning. Strangely enough, the very different kinds of anguish of Fulbert and Serge Kaniewsky had converged. The last blow that had struck Serge in Arnhem had finally laid him low. All his rage and fury had abated. There was no longer anything left within him but an immense despair—and on that terrain, he was sure to meet the inventor.

La Candeur was radiant, as was Vladimir, while Rouletabille was pensive. He had said: "It's still not proof. She might have entrusted herself to Monsieur Lixte, who must certainly have come in search of his wife, after having been told of her arrival in Holland. This Monsieur Lixte, to whom Nicole might have confided herself, who knows the Boche and what they're capable of, even outside their own country—remember how Nourry died—doubtless decided that it was preferable for Nicole to continue the comedy. Until we've caught up with them both, hope still remains to us."

Thus Rouletabille had spoken. Had anyone even heard him? The others made no reply. Did he even believe what he was saying himself?

The fact is that he said it without any great conviction. He was worn out. He had accomplished more than he had hoped, and he no longer dared, after an adventure that had saved Paris, to ask Providence for another favor, that would have saved Nicole as well.

He had moments, however, when it was as if he were awakened with a start by the vision of a gesture that he repeated mechanically. He believed himself, and felt himself, still in the process of striking Nicole! And he would have given his life not to have struck the true one!

Until reaching Arnhem, he had shown himself to be strong—stronger than he would have believed; he had thought that there, at least, the doubt would cease.

Well, the doubt was continuing...or, to put it more accurately, the hope, without having disappeared completely, was now very faint...very faint indeed...

In the train, he wept silently on seeing the distraught faces of Fulbert and Serge.

The Pole was no longer manifesting any hostility toward him. Docile, he allowed himself to be led, without any reaction. There was no longer anything but grief, in a corner...

In Rotterdam, they set forth in pursuit of Lixhe—or, rather, the all followed Rouletabille, who searched for Lixhe. From the editorial offices they were sent to the harbor; they were seen wandering there like souls in torment along the canals animated by traffic multiplied tenfold since the war, in spite of the hindrance of submarines. They stopped for lunch in an immense brasserie where Lixhe usually ate. The brasserie was also a kind of commercial center where a thousand deals were struck over anchovy stew and enormous tankards of beer. But Lixhe was not there.

Someone who knew Lixhe told them: "He left this morning for Flessingue."

They went to the police, who were also searching for them, and were told with certainty that Lixhe, who had been rejoined by his wife, a German prisoner for six months, had taken the train for Flessingue.

An hour later, they took the train for Flessingue.

They arrived in Flessingue just in time to see the ship carrying Lixhe and his wife leave.

Rouletabille said: "If, as I assume, Nicole has entrusted herself entirely to Lixhe, the latter, thinking Nicole insufficiently safe in Holland, has taken her to England.

They had to wait two days for a ship to England.

Serge and Fulbert were no longer talking to Rouletabille at all. They sometimes listened to him, but like people who did not hear or did not understand. They were no longer eating. They were no longer even weeping.

La Candeur and Vladimir went to play cards in cafés.

The nights were terrible for Rouletabille, who was no longer sleeping. As soon as he became drowsy, he saw himself murdering Nicole.

Finally, they embarked. The crossing was accomplished normally. They arrived in London and went to the police. There, they learned that Lixhe and his wife Barbara had just left for Liverpool.

Serge declared that he would not go to Liverpool, that he would no longer have the strength, for he was keeping what remained to him to go back to France, to see once again the places where he had loved Nicole, and to die. Fulbert wanted to go with Rouletabille to Liverpool.

"It's better," he said. "It will be more certain." And he began to laugh, and embrace Rouletabille.

Fulbert was on the brink of madness, so the reporter left him in London with Serge, under the protection of

La Candeur and Vladimir, who shut both of them in the same room and went to the bar to consume cocktails, whisky and brandy, while they played dice interminably. In England, Vladimir had become Rumanian again, on Rouletabille's advice.

When the latter reached Liverpool everyone told him that Monsieur and Madame Lixhe had embarked in Liverpool for America. This time, no further doubt was possible; there was nothing more to do than go back to Paris.

They went back to Paris.

Before arriving at the railway station, Rouletabille said to Serge and Fulbert: "One hope remains to us. If Lixhe, in order to save Nicole from the Boche police, has simulated a departure for America with her, they must both have left the steamship when it called in at Brest."

"In that case," said Serge, in a voice from beyond the grave, "we'll find Nicole in her mother's house."

"Possibly!" Rouletabille replied. "I've consulted the timetables. She might have arrived in Paris five hours ahead of us."

As soon as they disembarked in Paris, they climbed into a cab and were taken to Neuilly, to the Fulberts' home.

They did not find Nicole there. They did not even find Madame Fulbert. The house was locked up and the neighbors were unable to give them any useful information.

That was the final straw. The father and the fiancé fell into one another's arms.

Rouletabille left them embracing and, perhaps as desperate as them, climbed back into the cab. He did not even here the shouts of La Candeur and Vladimir. He set off at top sped.

He had give an address in the Rue de Saussaies—the address of the Sûreté Générale.

When he arrived here, however, he saw Vladimir and La Candeur leaping out of another cab, and Fulbert and Serge getting out behind them.

"We're not leaving you yet," said La Candeur. "We made them understand that if you left us like that, it was because you still had a glimmer of hope."

"None!" said Rouletabille. "None! It's finished. I've just come to make a report on my mission. I've succeeded in saving Paris, but I haven't succeeded in saving Nicole."

He crossed the courtyard in haste, and climbed the stairs. The other followed him. They had the habit by now of following him, and still nourishing, deep inside them, an impossible hope...

When they arrived in the vestibule of the head of the Sûreté Générale, they perceived, beside a man they did not know, Nicole and Madame Fulbert!

We shall not attempt to describe the scene that followed: the cries, the tears of joy, the delirium of that unexpected reunion.

"So it's you who was pursuing us," said the unknown man, who made himself known to them immediately, and who was none other than Monsieur Lixhe. "I thought we were dealing with Boche spies!"

In response to that joyful tumult, the door opened, and then, in the head of the Sûreté Générale's reception room, Rouletabille saw his editor and all the gentlemen from the famous secret cabinet meeting. They had gathered there to make a decision as to whether to advise

Parisians to evacuate the capital in the face of the urgent peril of the *Titania.*

Rouletabille went forward then, and, introducing Fulbert, Serge and Nicole to the gentlemen, cried: "I promised you that I would kill them or save them! My comrades and I have saved all three of them!"

To which Horn-rimmed Glasses said: "Well, I can tell you now that I haven't been so emotional since the Battle of the Marne."

The next day *L'Époque* appeared with a large headline:

IF THE MIRACLE OF THE MARNE SAVED FRANCE, PARIS HAS BEEN SAVED BY THE MIRACLE OF ROULETABILLE!

Afterword
Has Rouletabille Really Saved Paris?

The weakest element of *Rouletabille chez Krupp*, from a rational viewpoint, is the superweapon at its heart—a weakness inherent in the paradoxical nature of the motif. Because Leroux must have written the novel in a hurry—although it does show signs of secondary adjustment implying that it was probably completed in its entirety before he began work on *Le Sous-marin "Le Vengeur*," which was surely written in dribs and drabs while it was being serialized—and because it was to some extent a pioneering exercise, he clearly did not think through the consequences of introducing such a powerful device into a novel whose fundamental conceptual framework demands that the world within the text ultimately be left unchanged. For that reason, having devoted a good deal of narrative labor to inventing and characterizing the *Titania*, he eventually had to abandon it—almost to forget it—in order to contrive a suspenseful climax in which it does not feature, revolving around a problem which, in terms of the big picture initially sketched out, is of scant relevance.

As fictitious superweapons go, the *Titania* is rather unambitious. By 1917, several stories featuring nuclear weapons had already been published, and numerous stories extrapolating the power of mysterious rays akin to X-rays to apocalyptic proportions had also appeared. Leroux shows a deliberate restraint in deciding to set aside Professor Fulbert's adventures with radium and make the *Titania* a more conventional weapon: effectively a kind of massive cluster bomb, whose hypothetical lethal force merely combines the effects of existing explosive, incendiary and gas-bearing shells. He was, however, compelled by the demands of his plot to equip it with something unique that might serve as a pivotal secret whose revelation or suppression might temporarily divert the course of history.

Leroux's solution to that narrative difficulty—the notion of an automatic course-adjustment system, which makes his "torpedo" into a prototypical "homing missile"—is not without ingenuity, and certainly entitles him to marks for anticipatory acumen, but in terms of narrative currency, it is not really up to the job. Whatever the *L'Époque* headline that concludes, the story might say, a moment's thought would convince any reader that Rouletabille has not saved Paris at all. Far from it, in fact; if the novel's imaginative parameters are accepted, then Germany is logically bound to smash French resistance and win the war—and the Kaiser's reign as the literal Antichrist is about to begin.

The Germans have, after all, actually built the *Titania*, and have the means to fire it. All that they lack, we are told, is a sequence of numbers important to the functioning of its course-correction system. They will discover that the sequence they have been given is misleading when they carry out the tests scheduled to take place immediately after the escape of the three people who know the real sequence. Given that the sequence in question has been determined by the scientific method, however, there is no earthly reason why Krupp's engineers cannot work out what is wrong with the one they have been given, and correct it. And even if they cannot, why should that be fatal to the *Titania*'s chances of destroying Paris? Given that it can fly and explode, and sow destruction over such a wide area, is the pinpoint accuracy of its delivery so very important? If the purpose of the guidance mechanism is merely to correct for perturbations of the atmosphere, would it not be sufficient for the Germans merely to select a clear day on which to fire it? And even if it were not actually to land within the fortifications of Paris, or even its suburbs, is it not bound to do tremendous damage wherever it does land? At the most, the success of Rouletabille's project can have only served to delay the inevitable—although he might have contrived a longer delay had he taken better advantage of his seemingly-abundant opportunities for sabotage at the Krupp factory.

It is, however, arguable that looking at the problem—and, indeed, the entire novel—from the logical point of view is not the appropriate stance to take. The real narrative function of the *Titania* is not to investigate the question of whether a new innovation in weaponry might alter the course of the war decisively and conclusively in favor of one side or the other (as the invention of the atom bomb was to do in the American/Japanese War of 1943-1945) but to perform a symbolic function, in which the primary requirement is not so much its destructive potential as its sheer size. The essential feature of the *Titania* is that it *looks* colossal and awesome—that it is, in itself, a kind of *alter ego* of both the Kaiser and the Krupp armaments factory. Its defeat is similarly symbolic, and the logical objections raised in the previous paragraph are not really relevant in that context.

Similar considerations apply to such questions as why, if Rouletabille is the French government's "go-to guy" in a moment of national crisis, the poor fellow has been kicking his heels in the trenches for four years as a humble corporal, instead of serving as a field agent in the French Secret Service. His return journey from the trenches in the first chapter of the story is, in its fashion, just as symbolic as his tour of Krupp Hell or the climactic chase (during which the demands of narrative suspense require him unaccountably to forget how to use a telephone, as well as his urgent and imperious duty to report his success in extracting the mad scientist and the wobbly Pole from German hands to his own government). It is, however, the *Titania* that is the novel's central symbol and scarecrow-in-chief: the Kaiser, and everything the Kaiser stands for, *writ large*.

In the real world, of course, there are no weapons too dreadful to use, and it does not matter a damn whether the thread currently holding them over our head like the Sword of Damocles holds firm or not, because we are perfectly capable of destroying civilization, and ourselves, merely by continuing to squander the ecological and economic capital we have inherited—and, indeed, are well on the way to completing the job. There is nothing wrong, however, given such beleaguered circumstances, in a touch of nostalgia and escapism, which can take us back, temporarily, to a more innocent way of thinking, when we could still just about believe, if we only shut our eyes and tried hard enough, in miracles and heroes.

SF & FANTASY

Henri Allorge. *The Great Cataclysm*
Guy d'Armen. *Doc Ardan: The City of Gold and Lepers*
G.-J. Arnaud. *The Ice Company*
Charles Asselineau. *The Double Life*
Cyprien Bérard. *The Vampire Lord Ruthwen*
Aloysius Bertrand. *Gaspard de la Nuit*
Richard Bessière. *The Gardens of the Apocalypse*
Albert Bleunard. *Ever Smaller*
Félix Bodin. *The Novel of the Future*
Alphonse Brown. *City of Glass*
André Caroff. *The Terror of Madame Atomos; Miss Atomos; The Return of Madame Atomos; The Mistake of Madame Atomos; The Monsters of Madame Atomos; The Revenge of Madame Atomos*
Félicien Champsaur. *The Human Arrow; Ouha*
Didier de Chousy. *Ignis*
Captain Danrit. *Undersea Odyssey*
C. I. Defontenay. *Star (Psi Cassiopeia)*
Charles Derennes. *The People of the Pole*
Georges Dodds (anthologist). *The Missing Link*
Harry Dickson. *The Heir of Dracula*
Jules Dornay. *Lord Ruthven Begins*
Alfred Driou. *The Adventures of a Parisian Aeronaut*
Sâr Dubnotal *vs. Jack the Ripper*
Alexandre Dumas. *The Return of Lord Ruthven*
Renée Dunan. *Baal*
J.-C. Dunyach. *The Night Orchid; The Thieves of Silence*
Henri Duvernois. *The Man Who Found Himself*
Achille Eyraud. *Voyage to Venus*
Henri Falk. *The Age of Lead*
Paul Féval. *Anne of the Isles; Knightshade; Revenants; Vampire City; The Vampire Countess; The Wandering Jew's Daughter*
Paul Féval, *fils. Felifax, the Tiger-Man*
Charles de Fieux. *Lamékis*
Arnould Galopin. *Doctor Omega*; *Doctor Omega & The Shadowmen*
Léon Gozlan. *The Vampire of the Val-de-Grâce*
G.L. Gick. *Harry Dickson and the Werewolf of Rutherford Grange*
Edmond Haraucourt. *Illusions of Immortality*
Nathalie Henneberg. *The Green Gods*
V. Hugo, P. Foucher & P. Meurice. *The Hunchback of Notre-Dame*

Michel Jeury. *Chronolysis*
Gustave Kahn. *The Tale of Gold and Silence*
Gérard Klein. *The Mote in Time's Eye*
Louis-Guillaume de La Follie. *The Unpretentious Philosopher*
Jean de La Hire. *Enter the Nyctalope; The Nyctalope on Mars; The Nyctalope vs. Lucifer; The Nyctalope Steps In; Night of the Nyctalope*
Etienne-Léon de Lamothe-Langon. *The Virgin Vampire*
André Laurie. *Spiridon*
Gabriel de Lautrec. *The Vengeance of the Oval Portrait*
Alain le Drimeur. *The Future City*
Georges Le Faure & Henri de Graffigny. *The Extraordinary Adventures of a Russian Scientist Across the Solar System* (2 vols.)
Gustave Le Rouge. *The Vampires of Mars The Dominion of the World* (w/Gustave Guitton) (4 vols.)
Jules Lermina. *Mysteryville; Panic in Paris; To-Ho and the Gold Destroyers; The Secret of Zippelius*
Jean-Marc & Randy Lofficier. *Edgar Allan Poe on Mars; The Katrina Protocol; Pacifica; Robonocchio; Tales of the Shadowmen 1-9*
Xavier Mauméjean. *The League of Heroes*
Joseph Méry. *The Tower of Destiny*
Hippolyte Mettais. *The Year 5865*
Louise Michel. *The Human Microbes; The New World*
José Moselli. *Illa's End*
John-Antoine Nau. *Enemy Force*
Marie Nizet. *Captain Vampire*
C. Nodier, A. Beraud & Toussaint-Merle. *Frankenstein*
Henri de Parville. *An Inhabitant of the Planet Mars*
Gaston de Pawlowski. *Journey to the Land of the 4th Dimension*
Georges Pellerin. *The World in 2000 Years*
Ernest Pérochon. *The Frenetic People*
Pierre Pelot. *The Child Who Walked on the Sky*
J. Polidori, C. Nodier, E. Scribe. *Lord Ruthven the Vampire*
P.-A. Ponson du Terrail. *The Vampire and the Devil's Son*
Henri de Régnier. *A Surfeit of Mirrors*
Maurice Renard. *The Blue Peril; Doctor Lerne; The Doctored Man; A Man Among the Microbes; The Master of Light*
Jean Richepin. *The Wing; The Crazy Corner*
Albert Robida. *The Adventures of Saturnin Farandoul; The Clock of the Centuries; Chalet in the Sky*

J.-H. Rosny Aîné. *Helgvor of the Blue River; The Givreuse Enigma; The Mysterious Force; The Navigators of Space; Vamireh; The World of the Variants; The Young Vampire*
Marcel Rouff. *Journey to the Inverted World*
Han Ryner. *The Superhumans*
Brian Stableford. *The New Faust at the Tragicomique;The Empire of the Necromancers (The Shadow of Frankenstein; Frankenstein and the Vampire Countess; Frankenstein in London); Sherlock Holmes & The Vampires of Eternity; The Stones of Camelot; The Wayward Muse.* (anthologist) *The Germans on Venus; News from the Moon; The Supreme Progress; The World Above the World; Nemoville; Investigations of the Future*
Jacques Spitz. *The Eye of Purgatory*
Kurt Steiner. *Ortog*
Eugène Thébault. *Radio-Terror*
C.-F. Tiphaigne de La Roche. *Amilec*
Théo Varlet. *The Golden Rock. The Xenobiotic Invasion; Timeslip Troopers* (w/André Blandin); *The Martian Epic* (w/Octave Joncquel)
Paul Vibert. *The Mysterious Fluid*
Villiers de l'Isle-Adam. *The Scaffold; The Vampire Soul*
Philippe Ward. *Artahe*
Philippe Ward & Sylvie Miller. *The Song of Montségur*

MYSTERIES & THRILLERS

M. Allain & P. Souvestre. *The Daughter of Fantômas*
A. Anicet-Bourgeois, Lucien Dabril. *Rocambole*
A. Bernède. *Belphegor*; *Judex* (w/Louis Feuillade)
A. Bisson & G. Livet. *Nick Carter vs. Fantômas*
V. Darlay & H. de Gorsse. *Lupin vs. Holmes: The Stage Play*
Paul Féval. *Gentlemen of the Night; John Devil; The Black Coats ('Salem Street; The Invisible Weapon; The Parisian Jungle; The Companions of the Treasure; Heart of Steel; The Cadet Gang; The Sword-Swallower)*
Emile Gaboriau. *Monsieur Lecoq*
Goron & Emile Gautier. *Spawn of the Penitentiary*
Steve Leadley. *Sherlock Holmes: The Circle of Blood*
Maurice Leblanc. *Arsène Lupin vs. Countess Cagliostro; Lupin vs. Holmes (The Blonde Phantom; The Hollow Needle); The Many Faces of Arsène Lupin*

Gaston Leroux. *Chéri-Bibi; The Phantom of the Opera; Rouletabille & the Mystery of the Yellow Room Rouletabille at Krupp's*
Richard Marsh. *The Complete Adventures of Judith Lee*
William Patrick Maynard. *The Terror of Fu Manchu; The Destiny of Fu Manchu*
Frank J. Morlock. *Sherlock Holmes: The Grand Horizontals; Sherlock Holmes vs Jack the Ripper*
Antonin Reschal. *The Adventures of Miss Boston*
P. de Wattyne & Y. Walter. *Sherlock Holmes vs. Fantômas*
David White. *Fantômas in America*

SCREENPLAYS

Mike Baron. *The Iron Triangle*
Emma Bull & Will Shetterly. *Nightspeeder; War for the Oaks*
Gerry Conway & Roy Thomas. *Doc Dynamo*
Steve Englehart. *Majorca*
James Hudnall. *The Devastator*
Jean-Marc & Randy Lofficier. *Royal Flush*
J.-M. & R. Lofficier & Marc Agapit. *Despair*
J.-M. & R. Lofficier & Joël Houssin. *City*
Andrew Paquette. *Peripheral Vision*
Robert L. Robinson, Jr. *Judex*
R. Thomas, J. Hendler & L. Sprague de Camp. *Rivers of Time*

NON-FICTION

Stephen R. Bissette. *Blur 1-5. Green Mountain Cinema 1; Teen Angels*
Win Scott Eckert. *Crossovers* (2 vols.)
Jean-Marc & Randy Lofficier. *Shadowmen* (2 vols.)
Randy Lofficier. *Over Here*

HEXAGON COMICS

Franco Frescura & Luciano Bernasconi. *Wampus*
Franco Frescura & Giorgio Trevisan. *CLASH*
L. Bernasconi, J.-M. Lofficier & Juan Roncagliolo Berger. *Phenix*
Claude Legrand, J.-M. Lofficier & L. Bernasconi. *Kabur*

Franco Oneta. *Zembla*
L. Buffolente, Lofficier & J.-J. Dzialowski. *Strangers: Homicron*
Danilo Grossi. *Strangers: Jaydee*
Claude Legrand & Luciano Bernasconi. *Strangers: Starlock*

ART BOOKS

Jean-Pierre Normand. *Science Fiction Illustrations*
Raven Okeefe. *Raven's L'il Critters; Rave's Faves*
Randy Lofficier & Raven Okeefe. *If Your Possum Go Daylight...*
Daniele Serra. *Illusions*